MMXV

THE WHITE REVIEW

EDITORS — BENJAMIN EASTHAM & JACQUES TESTARD
DESIGN, ART DIRECTION — RAY O'MEARA
POETRY EDITOR — J. S. TENNANT
US EDITOR — TYLER CURTIS
ASSISTANT EDITOR — FRANCESCA WADE
EDITORIAL ASSISTANT — HARRY THORNE
DESIGN ASSISTANT — GABRIELLA VOYIAS

CONTRIBUTING EDITORS — JACOB BROMBERG, LAUREN ELKIN, EMMELINE FRANCIS,
PATRICK LANGLEY, BELLA MARRIN, DANIEL MEDIN,
SAM SOLNICK, EMILY STOKES, KISHANI WIDYARATNA

ADVERTISING — LUCIE ELVEN

HONORARY TRUSTEES — MICHAEL AMHERST, DEREK ARMSTRONG, HUGUES DE DIVONNE,
SIMON FAN, NIALL HOBHOUSE, CATARINA LEIGH-PEMBERTON,
MICHAEL LEUE, TOM MORRISON-BELL, AMY POLLNER,
CÉCILE DE ROCHEQUAIRIE, EMMANUEL ROMAN, HUBERT TESTARD,
MICHEL TESTARD, GORDON VENEKLASEN,
DANIELA & RON WILLSON, CAROLINE YOUNGER

COVER ART BY PATRICIA TREIB
PRINTED BY PUSH, LONDON
PAPER BY ANTALIS MCNAUGHTON (OLIN CREAM 100GSM, OLIN WHITE SMOOTH 120GSM)
BESPOKE PAPER MARBLE BY PAYHEMBURY MARBLE PAPERS
TYPESET IN JOYOUS (BLANCHE)

PUBLISHED BY THE WHITE REVIEW, MARCH 2015
EDITION OF 1,500
ISBN No. 978-0-9927562-4-6

THE WHITE REVIEW, 243 KNIGHTSBRIDGE, LONDON SW7 1DN
WWW.THEWHITEREVIEW.ORG

Supported using public funding by
ARTS COUNCIL
ENGLAND
LOTTERY FUNDED

CONTENTS

CONTENTS

APPENDIX

Cover:
GREEN SHAPE (2014) by PATRICIA TREIB

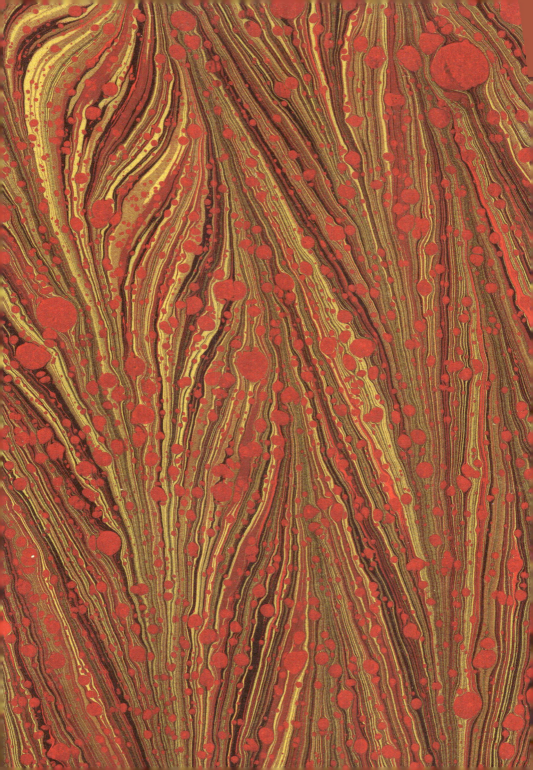

FOREWORD

GUIDANCE FOR YOUNG POETS

We suggest you do not send us:

Poems about barnacles;

Poems featuring characters in sombreros or in vitro fertilisation;

Poems that that make a pun on Eid and IEDs;

Poems with titles like 'Auspices of Transience', or using the words 'the infinite' or 'infinity';

Poems written in Microsoft Word by Microsoft Office;

[N.B. Crazy font: crazy person; coloured font: crazy person with good intentions]

Poems on euthanasia or in rhetorical questions;

Poems that liken people to broken records;

Poems written in East Berlin cafés;

Poems in italics; about Chechens; titled 'Untitled';

Poems likening breasts to epigrams;

Poems about the cosmos, viscera, chill winds, desolation, witches' Sabbaths;

Poems in the voice of Uri Geller or Josef Fritzl;

Poems 'after' Kurt Schwitters.

Thank you.

STRANGELY OPPRESSIVE FREEDOM

BY

JON DAY

> Consider the cyclist as he passes, the supreme specialist, transfiguring that act of moving from place to place which is itself the sentient body's supreme specialty. He is the term of locomotive evolution from slugs and creeping things.
>
> Hugh Kenner, SAMUEL BECKETT

Bicycle couriering is difficult, dangerous work. Couriers are paid for piecework and employed as self-employed subcontractors, meaning there's no sick pay, no employment protection, no pension scheme. You earn only what you ride for. If you're injured while working your employers have no obligation to you. Apart from the assistance of the London Courier Emergency Fund – a grass-roots organisation run by couriers that pays out small amounts to riders injured on the job – you're on your own.

Physically, the work is grindingly difficult. On an average day you'll cycle sixty to one hundred miles, deliver twenty or so packages, and earn maybe three pounds per package. On a good day you'll break £100. On a fixed-gear bike like mine, with a gearing of 49/17, that amounts to around 29,000 complete pedal revolutions per day. On an average day you'll earn 0.003p for each turn of the cranks. On slow days you often earn far less than minimum wage. You're largely ignored, if not disdained, by the people you work for. Like other dangerous work it fosters a strong sense of community, an informal support network focused on races, drinking, and listening to interminable stories about bad controlling or those one-off, impossibly lucrative jobs and satisfying runs.

I had a choice, of course, when many people don't, but for me the sheer joy of being physically tired at the end of a day's work was a revelation. In THE SOUL OF LONDON, Ford Madox Ford described labour in London as divided fairly equally between that of the mind and that of the body. 'Workers in London,' he wrote, 'divide themselves, roughly, into those who sell the labour of their bodies and those who sell their attentions. You see men in the streets digging trenches, pulling stout wires out of square holes in pavements, pecking away among greasy vapours at layers of asphalt, scattering shovelfuls of crushed gravel under the hoofs of slipping horses and under the crunching tyres of wheels. If walls would fall out of offices you would see paler men and women adding up the records of money paid to these others. That, with infinite variations, is work in London.'

Since Ford's time the balance has altered, and labour in London, as in many post-industrial cities, has become predominantly cerebral or service-based. For me couriering felt like one of the few ways left in the city to work with my body. Through cycling miles and miles each day I got to know it alongside the city. I learned how much food and water it needed to run smoothly, how it performed in the heat or in the rain. I learned its limits, its cul-de-sacs and alleyways, alongside those of London.

Increasingly, the lives of our bodies have become disciplined, made to conform to the stranglehold of nine–to–five existence. One of the reasons walking has become such a popular topic for writers is that physical exertion is nowadays often isolated from everyday being. Mostly, the needs of our bodies are allowed to announce them–selves only at prearranged times: during the regularly scheduled run or gym appoint–ment.

In *WANDERLUST* Rebecca Solnit argues that people have forgotten about their bodies, forgotten that they are more than mere vehicles for minds, passive vessels to be inhabited by our all-important egos. We have forgotten that our bodies 'could be adequate to the challenges that face them and a pleasure to use,' she writes; we 'per–ceive and imagine [our] bodies as essentially passive, a treasure or a burden but not a tool for work and travel.' What Solnit calls the 'vital body in action' has been largely misplaced in post-industrial society: lost to a world of digital distraction or annexed to the contained and constraining fields of 'work' and 'play'. A Heideggerian notion of being-in-the-world has been replaced with the feeling that we experience reality only through and within a variety of tightly controlled spaces: cars, cubicles, and offices. Couriering reminded me about the existence of my body. Daily I felt the delicious burn of muscles, the faintness of pure hunger and sugar crashes – 'meeting', as rac–ing cyclists put it, 'the man with the hammer' – and the deep pleasure of slaking real thirst. After a year on the road couriering ceased to feel like a temporary job, a stopgap between university courses and some still unknown career, and became all-consuming. I got sucked in.

¶ For most of the twentieth century the bicycle was explicitly associated with work. The on-yer-bikism of Norman Tebbit merely reflected a more deep-seated asso–ciation between the self-propelled movement of cycling and labour: of pedalling to work as work. It was partly for this reason that, at the turn of the century, English socialists seized on the bicycle as a vehicle for political agitation. The *CLARION*, a left-wing newspaper founded in 1891, started life as a socialist cycling club, and later its members would deliver the paper by bicycle. In Italy, communists founded a group called the 'Red Cyclists' to campaign for 'cheap bikes for the working classes', while manufacturers tried to cash in on the socialist revolution of cycling by producing a bicycle tyre branded the 'Karl Marx'. For the Red Cyclists, writes the historian John Foot, the symbolism was obvious: 'to pedal was to work. The bike was the "vehicle of the poor" and the "ally of their effort."'

In the professional peloton of the heroic era of bicycle racing, too, the bicycle represented labour. Professional cyclists still aren't paid a great deal, especially those who aren't famous, but before the Second World War a bicycle race represented an opportunity: a chance for poor farm hands to break away from the constraints of their lives. 'A racing cyclist, at least in the old days,' writes Foot 'was a worker: one who did, and was paid a wage based on the races they won, on how well they performed.' Much like couriering, racing was paid as piecework. In the early years of road cycling, before doping was made illegal, before the trade teams and the sponsored coddling, before the hyper–tactical machinations of the contemporary sport, 'cyclists were individuals battling against the elements and the limits imposed by their own bodies,' writes Foot. Racing itself was heavily politicised. For those on the left of the political spectrum – both writers and riders – the peloton was interpreted as a socialist utopia, a field of common endeavour within which racers could help each other out or show solidarity by neutralising the race, or providing aerodynamic cover for their stars. For the right the race represented the triumph of individual exceptionalism.

In Luigi Bartolini's 1946 novel BICYCLE THIEVES, made into a film in 1948 by Vittorio De Sica, the bicycle becomes a symbol of escape from the poverty of postwar Italy. A poor unemployed man named Antonio is offered a job delivering and putting up posters around Rome. The job stipulates that he must provide his own bicycle, and so his wife Maria sells her best bed linen to reclaim the bike Antonio has previously pawned. On his first day of work his bicycle is stolen from under his nose and, accompanied by his son Bruno, Antonio embarks on a kind of cyclogeographic tour of Rome's less salubrious quarters to reclaim it.

The film is a quest narrative. Antonio and Bruno follow strangers through the crowds, they search for parts of his bicycle at Piazza Vittorio market, where dealers spread their deconstructed machines in front of them like piles of fruit. They find a bicycle that they think is Antonio's and alert a passing policeman, but the serial numbers don't match. They visit a workingman's chapel and are forced to endure a sermon before continuing their search. At one point they give up all hope of finding the bike and, drunk with despair, Antonio spends the last of his money on a slap–up lunch in an upmarket trattoria. Eventually, desperate to keep the job which was to provide an escape from poverty, Antonio himself becomes a bicycle thief. He is quickly apprehended, but the man whose bicycle he has stolen notices Bruno and, in a moment of compassion, pardons Antonio, who is left to walk home forlornly with his son. BICYCLE THIEVES is about the desperations of poverty, but it is also a meditation on the bicycle as a vehicle for self–determination through work. It's a film I often thought about as I cycled around the city.

¶ The association of the bicycle with labour during the mid–twentieth century was partly born of its curious hybridity as a machine. Cyclists' bodies are subdued to their instruments, and riding another person's bike often feels intensely alien. It is a cliché that the bike, of all tools, can become an extension of the body, but nonetheless true for that. After a while you begin to worry about your bike as though it is a part of you. Anxiously you check the small areola of rust surrounding the hole at the bottom of the chromed seat stays; the notch in the headset giving your steering a slight bias; the creak of the wheel where you've cracked a spoke.

Many writers have reflected on the neatness of the Cartesian metaphor of bicycle and rider as body and mind, as dualist parts of a unified whole. At the dawn of the cycling era the strange logic of the bicycle – the way in which cycling creates a prosthetic relation between person and machine – was seized upon in particular by Futurist and modernist writers and artists, invested as they were in the triumph of the mechanical over the mental, or at least, in a future where human inadequacies could be engineered away by the application of reason. For these writers the conceit was obvious: people didn't ride bicycles, bicycles rode people. The bike was a symbol of Man multiplied by machine.

In one of his Futurist manifestos F. T. Marinetti associated the bicycle with other emerging technologies, prophesying the deranging stimulants of the mechanical age:

> Those people who today make use of the telegraph, the telephone, the phonograph, the train, the bicycle, the motorcycle, the automobile, the ocean liner, the dirigible, the aeroplane, the cinema, the great newspaper (synthesis of a day in the world's life) do not realise that these various means of communication, transportation and information have a decisive influence on their psyches.

Like Marinetti, the artist Fernand Léger interpreted the act of cycling as the coming together of body and machine, but also as a form of art. 'A bicycle operates in the realm of light,' he wrote, 'it takes control of legs, arms and body, which move on it, by it and under it. Rounded thighs become pistons, which rise or fall, fast or slow.' The threat to autonomy associated with industrialised labour was prefigured by the threat to the individual will demonstrated by the bicycle.

The French playwright and poet Alfred Jarry, founder of the playfully counter-intuitive discipline of 'Pataphysics' – which he defined as 'the science of imaginary solutions' – called the bicycle Man's 'external skeleton', and rode a state-of-the-art Clement machine running the impossibly high gear ratio of 36/9, so that his wheels revolved four times for every turn of his pedals.

Jarry saw the bicycle as the epitome of Pataphysical technology. As he rode around Paris he would let off a pair of pistols to deter attacking dogs, and he later scandalised society by wearing his cycling outfit to the funeral of the poet Stéphane Mallarmé. When he died Jarry left an unpaid bill for bicycle repairs which would eventually bankrupt his sister. She died soon after.

Cycling, and the image of mechanised hybridity it provided, was central to Jarry's writing. In his short story 'The Crucifixion Considered as a Downhill Bicycle Race' he rewrote the passion of the Christ in the breathless High Style of newspaper reports that described the newly inaugurated Tour de France:

> Jesus got away to a good start. In those days, according to the excellent sports commentator
> St. Matthew, it was customary to flagellate the sprinters at the start the way a coachman
> whips his horses. The whip both stimulates and gives a hygienic massage. Jesus, then, got
> off in good form, but he had a flat right away. A bed of thorns punctured the whole cir-
> cumference of his front tyre.

Four years before his death, Jarry wrote his last novel, THE SUPERMALE. In it he described a 10,000-mile race between a group of cyclists and a train, the riders fuelled
by a mysterious 'perpetual motion food' made up of strychnine and alcohol. During
the race one rider dies but is contractually obligated to finish the race. For Jarry bicycle and body formed a self-sustaining system: the legs were massaged by the act of
pedalling; the body self-lubricated as sweat gathered between the thighs:

> Complex nervous and muscular systems enjoy absolute rest, it seems to me, while their
> 'counterpart' works. We know that, for a bicyclist, each leg in turn rests, and even benefits
> from a massage that is automatic, and as restorative as any embrocation, while the other
> leg is doing the work.

Bound by metal rods to their machines, the five-man crew cycle from Paris to Asia
paced by flying machines, reaching speeds of 300 kilometres an hour. THE SUPER-
MALE pointed towards a disturbing future in which the body would be utterly dehu-
manised by the bicycle, enslaved by the machines that had once promised freedom.
   Samuel Beckett too was obsessed with the deranged metaphysics of cycling, with
the philosophical lessons that could be learnt from the saddle. According to the critic
Hugh Kenner, Godot himself was an avatar for 'Monsieur Godeau', a French national
champion cyclist who typified 'Cartesian man in excelsis'. For Beckett the bicycle
represented the triumph of what Kenner calls 'the simple machines' – lever, pulley,
gear – over man in a state of nature:

> To consider the endless perfection of the chain, the links forever settling about the cogs, is
> a perpetual pleasure; to reflect that a specified link is alternately stationary with respect
> to the sprocket, then in motion with respect to the same sprocket, without hiatus between
> these conditions, is to entertain the sort of soothing mystery which . . . you can study all
> your life and not understand. The wheels are a miracle; the contraption moves on air, sus-
> tained by a network of wires in tension not against gravity but against one another.

Many of Beckett's characters are dependent on the material crutch of their bicycles for support. In *MORE PRICKS THAN KICKS*, Belacqua Shuah forgoes his human companion when he spots a bicycle lying in a field, before stealing it, lying down in the grass with it, and attempting to make love to it. When Molloy is separated from his bicycle he breaks down, starts staggering around in circles and eventually becomes unable to walk, so pulls himself along on his belly using his crutches before rolling into a ditch. In Watt, the eponymous character dreams of bicycles as he enters the house of Knott. Beckett's bikes, like Jarry's, are often sinister objects. In *MERCIER AND CAMIER* he wrote 'the bicycle is a great good. But it can turn nasty, if ill employed.' His prose evokes the bicycle at the level of the sentence too, filled as it is with its cyclical rhythms: those emergent, flowing sentences animated by short–term repetitions: a ratchet–prose ramping up momentum and significance with each turn of the cranks.

Beckett's fellow Irish author Flann O'Brien was an equally visionary cyclist–mystic. In the cyclical hell of *THE THIRD POLICEMAN* he documented the curious psychosexual relationship that could develop between people and bicycles from within the confines of a profoundly strange detective novel. According to O'Brien's 'Atomic Theory', over time cyclists begin to merge with their machines due to the exchange of atoms between the two. The unnamed narrator of *THE THIRD POLICEMAN* communes with his bike, becoming one with it as they traverse the bad roads of the purgatorial Parish:

> How can I convey the perfection of my comfort on the bicycle, the completeness of my union with her, the sweet responses she gave me at every particle of her frame? I felt that I had known her for many years and that she had known me and that we understood each other utterly [...] I passed my hand with unintended tenderness – sensuously indeed – across the saddle [...] It was a gentle saddle yet calm and courageous [...] Her saddle seemed to spread invitingly into the most enchanting of all seats while her two handlebars, floating finely with the wild grace of alighting wings, beckoned to me to lend my mastery for free and joyful journeyings, the lightest of light running in the company of the swift ground to safe havens far away, the whir of the true front wheel in my ear as it spun perfectly beneath my clear eye and the strong fine back wheel with unadmired industry raising gently dust on the dry roads. How desirable her seat was, how charming the invitation of her slim encircling handlebars, how unaccountably competent and reassuring her pump resting warmly against her rear thigh.

In O'Brien's novel the bicycle is given volition, becoming a character in its own right. With his 'Atomic Theory' O'Brien argued (with the pub–bore's grasp of particle physics) that the constant exchange of atoms between Man and bicycle would eventually affect the psychology of each. And the process wasn't just one way. Not only do bikes in *THE THIRD POLICEMAN* become endowed with humanity, humanity takes on a latent bicyclosity. Cyclists begin to sleep in corridors propped up against walls on one elbow. At rest they stand with one foot on the curb and one in the gutter. Bicycles begin to steal from pantries: crumbs and tyre marks betraying this nocturnal activity. There are hints of more sinister activity, of bicycle rapes and murders. 'Of course there are other things connected with ladies and ladies' bicycles that I will mention to you separately some time,' reports Sergeant Pluck, the friendliest of the three titular policemen, 'but the man–charged bicycle is a phenomenon of great charm and intensity and a very dangerous article.'

❡ I wanted to talk to someone about the long–term effects of couriering, about what it felt like to do the job for a decade or more, to think about it not as a stop–gap but as a career, or a calling of some kind. I wanted to know what couriers do when they retire. And so I sought out someone who'd been on the road for a while and got out without succumbing to the dark predictions of O'Brien's Atomic Theory of cycling.

'Buffalo' Bill Chidley is a messengers' messenger. He started working as a courier in the early 80s, 'when you could make real money on the road', and when a fledgling courier sub–culture – all dreadlocks, tattoos, and tiny cycling hats – was beginning to emerge. The bicycle courier became a recognisable social type in the 80s, he recalls, immortalised in the children's cartoon STREETWISE and then, later, as 'Tyres', the rave–haunted courier in the sitcom SPACED. Bill retired after a decade in the saddle, and now works as a controller and edits MOVING TARGET, a bicycle messenger fanzine. He still looks like a courier. Keys jangle from his belt. He wears a huge bag, jeans rolled at the ankle and clip–in cycling shoes. Journalists seek him out for comment on the London cycling scene. Couriers doff their caps as he passes them in the street. I knew him as a controller, and met up with him to ask about the origins of London bicycle couriering, and about what happens when you give up the job.

We met in a pub in Islington filled with a few couriers and controllers reminiscing about their time on the road. Most of them said they had become controllers because they'd been couriers and didn't know what to do when their knees gave out, or when the work began to feel too mind–numbingly futile to continue. One of the older riders drinking with them, Mike, told me he'd recently given up couriering because he was waiting for an operation on his arthritic knees. He missed the job, he said, but was keeping himself busy as a dog walker, trying to work out what to do next. He said he'd probably get back in the saddle once he'd had the operation. He couldn't think of what else to do.

Like most controllers, Bill talks with fondness and nostalgia about the job. He misses the money, the freedom, and the fact that as a courier you're paid to ride your bike for a living. Most of all he missed the City, he told me, 'I hate the City police, but I love the City.' He misses knowing London in that intimate way that is the privilege of the courier. He knew it these days on screen, or from the pages of the A–Z. 'I still reckon that, apart from the people who are actually doing the Knowledge, couriers know the city best,' he said.

The first recognisable bicycle courier companies in London emerged in the 8os, Bill told me. Before that minicab companies touted for whatever business there was, and the industry was mainly controlled by gangsters. 'You get a lot of talk about the cab wars in the 7os,' Bill said, 'where cab drivers from different firms fought for business. I heard talk of people going over and taking shotguns to taxi ranks. There used to be a company that trained couriers, and they traced the birth of modern couriers to the postal strike of '74. But black cabs were being used to move stuff around before then. They talk about soldiers and prostitutes as the oldest jobs. I would put messengers before them.'

I asked him if working conditions had got worse since he first started the job, if couriers earn less money these days. He said they had and they do. 'It's not like when I was on the road, in the 8os. Then *everything* needed to be sent physically. We were delivering tapes to radio stations, to TV stations. Display ad copy to Fleet Street.' When I asked him why he thinks couriers have managed to cling on against a backdrop of technological change he stressed the human component of the business. 'It's not so much that we're quicker than the internet', Bill said, 'there's also a question of security. If you don't actually have a physical private cable and you have something sensitive to send across town you need to use a courier. When they were filming *LORD OF THE RINGS* I heard they had a private cable that came out at Pinewood. If they needed to do something with it in Soho, they weren't going to send that over the Internet. They had a private cable, hard-wired in. Nowadays we're moving hard drives around too. When they cut it really fine, then we end up moving the hard drives to the cinemas to screen the films.'

Bill's retired to the office now, away from the wind and the rain, from the weather and the city. He makes his money sending other riders to jobs. 'What do you make on us? Double?' I asked him. 'No, generally not. If we've got a vanilla job, where there's no discount, then we're making double, yeah. But there are so few of them. As a courier you're just above cleaners and just below security in the pecking order. We're an office service, so we'll tender. We'll go in and the opening gambit of our salespeople will be "Here are our prices, and today we're offering ten per cent off." Everything is negotiable, but the clients have to ask us first. Desperate companies drive the prices down for everyone. "Whatever they're doing it for we'll do it for less."'

We spoke about knowing London, about the uniqueness of the city experienced from the saddle. 'I learned London, more or less, from the tube map,' Bill said. 'You've got all these lines, and all this blank space in between. You've got this white space, and on a bike you fill in the gaps. I was born in London. But it's only when you look at the map, and you can see the railway lines, the river, that you realise how it all works. If you take somewhere like Fulham, it's actually an island. You've got the A4 across the top; you've got the river, and then these developments. Planning is supposed to make the city legible, but it doesn't.' As a controller you only really get to know the places in which your clients are based, he said. 'Some guys have been on the road for ten years and still only know Soho. Riders from my company used to have this reputation: if someone saw you east of Kingsway they'd say "The West End's that way, are you lost or something?"'

Now Bill lives through his maps, on the screen and through the radio. 'If I actu- ally go out now and ride around, I get lost. As a courier I got bored riding round in London because by the end I couldn't get lost; you know where everything is. I went through a phase where I deliberately tried to get lost, because London's so big that the idea of knowing where you are all the time is so overwhelming. But when you arrive at a point where you can't get lost it becomes boring. Now I go out and the physical structure of the city has changed quite a bit. So it's become interesting again. But I still think that, even though I've been off the road twelve years, my knowledge is better now. I'm constantly looking at a map. Always looking at a map.'

Couriering was attractive to me, as it was to Bill, because it was easy to know you weren't exploiting anyone when you were the one being exploited. The market place is brutally efficient. Unionisation has proved almost impossible in an industry so dependent on migrant labour. Whole fleets are sacked and replaced overnight. 'There were several attempts to unionise in the 80s,' Bill said, 'but you could never push it over the line. Partly because there was always this kind of "we don't need a union" feeling. People were like "we're professional couriers", but now they're on minimum wage. The companies have managed to pit all the couriers against each other. As a controller I see the other side of it. If I can't cover a job I'm fucked. It only works if I can persuade you to do the job – come on, you know, do this for me. What I need is for everyone to help each other and trust that it'll work out.'

I asked Bill if he missed the work. 'Yeah, every day. What I miss is being out- side. I ride to work and then I sit indoors. What I always miss is the sky. That's what I would be constantly looking at. You're always looking at it and asking is it going to rain? That's what I miss the most. Mostly London's weather is mediocre, but it changes. Don't like the weather now? Just wait half an hour. A new front will roll in.'

Finally we talked about leaving the job, about how to get out. It seems tricky for many. Maybe couriering makes you sad or maybe it attracts sad people to it – the endorphins generated by exercise providing a form of subtle self-medication – but it's true that many couriers have a touch of melancholia about them. Despite the dangers, in the seven years since I first began riding a bike for a living in London I have known more couriers to have committed suicide than to have died on the road. The isolation of the job can exacerbate despair and depression. The lack of structure, each

E

day drifting into the next, becoming a never-ending cycle with no apparent way out, eats away at you after a while. Career-couriers can easily succumb to the repetitiveness. Denied the enforced daily contact of office work, you can easily slip through the social bonds of the road to exist in a solipsistic vacuum. Then you become an eternal observer, your only social interaction coming from the brief and cursory points of contact with people at pick up and delivery, and the disembodied presence of the controller on the radio. It is easy to lose touch with things.

A few years ago I heard that a courier had committed suicide after having been stopped for running a red light. The cursory name check the police ran revealed an unpaid debt in Poland and a one-year prison sentence passed in absentia. Faced with deportation, with the loss of a life struggled for and cultivated into stability, he killed himself. He left behind his girlfriend and their young daughter.

¶ London writers have always been drawn to the idea of hard work in a city that seems ever more dependent on brainwork. As manual labour in the city has declined, so writers have become interested in cataloguing and recording the work of the body. By George Orwell's time there was already, he wrote, a 'sort of fetish of manual work' abroad in the city:

> We see a man cutting down a tree, and we make sure that he is filling a social need, just because he uses his muscles; it does not occur to us that he may only be cutting down a beautiful tree to make room for a hideous statue.

Much London writing has been obsessed with the secret history of working places, with the stories of those labouring shades who once walked and lived and worked in them. Often this interest was based on hands-on experience. Charles Dickens worked in a blacking factory as a child, a period in his life he remained deeply ashamed of. In LONDON LABOUR AND THE LONDON POOR Henry Mayhew outlined a fine-grained typology of work in the city, identifying the various castes of workers who used to keep London functioning: the mudlarks, costermongers, scavengers, and 'wandering tribes' who plied their trades on the streets of the city. In distinguishing the 'wanderers and the settlers', Mayhew wrote 'the nomad is then distinguished from the civilised man by his repugnance to regular and continuous labour – by his want of providence in laying up a store for the future – by his inability to perceive consequences ever so slightly removed from immediate apprehension – by his passion for stupefying herbs and roots and, where possible, for intoxicating fermented liquors – by his extraordinary powers of enduring privation – by his comparative insensibility to pain.' It is a fair definition of the cycle courier.

More recently, in the work of authors like Iain Sinclair, Peter Ackroyd and Rachel

Lichtenstein, the idea of work as a part of the identity of urban space still seems to be central. Yet the impulse to account for this lost labour is in some respects an attempt to address the new blandness that lies at the heart of the contemporary city, with its economy dominated by service industry jobs. The labour-fetishism of much London writing has itself been diagnosed as the nostalgic result of the decline of manual labour in the city, and of the architecture associated with it: with the docks and the factories which were once London's biggest employers. In *LONDON FROM PUNK TO BLAIR* Phil Baker argues that the notion of a secret city, lying parallel to the one most of us know, has always inspired London writers, but that:

> [the] value of the urban secret changes from era to era. The great secret of the nineteenth century was the extent of poverty and degradation, giving rise to revelatory books such as William Booth's *IN DARKEST LONDON* (1880). But by the end of the hyper-transparent late twentieth century, the secret was positive, and it was desired as never before. This desire for secret places relates to perennial fantasies of places 'off the map', like De Quincey's London *terrae incognitae*, and of liminal zones and glimpsed paradises – in the fictions of Alain-Fournier, H. G. Wells and Arthur Machen, for example – but it gains a new, belated urgency in over-developed, overexposed millennial London.

The writer James Heartfield argues that the manual labourer now forms part of a secret lost race of 'troglodytes' that haunt the contemporary city 'cleared away in the transformation of London into a city dedicated primarily to business services and retail'. Such nostalgia is symptomatic of a larger cultural project, represented in the work-porn of television programmes such as *DEADLIEST CATCH* and *TRAWLERMEN*, documenting hard work and its associated dangers for our voyeuristic pleasure.

Now cycle couriering too is implicated in this decline, and is increasingly seen as a dying trade. The narrative is familiar to all couriers, whether they subscribe to it or not. Since the advent of fax and email couriers have been living at the end of days. The bike, once the 'friend of the poor' and the 'ally of their effort' is losing its proletarian edge. It has been re-appropriated, not as a tool for work but as a vehicle for leisure.

Of course, regardless of the politics, everyone *should* be cycling more, and driving less. The notion that cycling is or should be the preserve of a dwindling and 'authentic' courier crowd, let alone that of the Critical Mass riders, naked cyclists and bike punks who see each revolution of the wheel as one more turn towards the greater revolution, is as alienating as it is wrong-headed. But on the final reckoning bike politics doesn't amount to much of anything. The fact is that most working people still prefer the underground. The cult of simplicity surrounding cycling has corresponded exactly to the decline of public infrastructure that most people use to get to work. Indeed in most cities the bicycle selfishly profits from this decline, gaining an advantage as traffic snarls up and trains fill up.

The central paradox of the labour of cycle couriering, therefore, is its strangely oppressive freedom. Many couriers revel in the fact that they can come and go as they please, that they work alone in the city on their own terms, that they can wear what they like and drink, smoke and take drugs all day without getting sacked. In reality of course you're the lowest in the economic food chain – capitalism's foot-soldiers, paid to pass the parcel around a massive financial circuit. And yet still the meteoric rise of the bicycle, reclaimed not as a tool of work but of leisure, continues. In an age of austerity, the underground systems of London and New York are literally grinding to-wards collapse. Meanwhile for a politician eager for popularity, nothing is easier than taking a can of paint and siphoning off a portion of tarmac for a bike lane. The class of people this pleases is small but increasingly vocal, highly visible in parts of the city where they were once scarce and oblivious to what was once a truth: increased cycling is a sign of decreased employment. When a bike shop appears in a depressed neighbourhood, you can be sure it's on the verge of gentrification.

Where I live in east London, the bicycle shop has become a destination in itself. Boutique bike shops serve coffee and cake whilst the mechanics, stars of the show, fix bicycles in the middle of the room while everyone watches. The nostalgia can also be seen in the bikes people choose to ride. In the 90s, Bill tells me, most couriers rode fat-tubed mountain bikes bristling with gears. Now there's been a turn towards the simple honesty of the fixed-gear track bicycle, with its single gear, its perpetually revolving pedals, its decent and uncluttered lack of brakes. Leather saddles riveted together with copper pins adorn these simple machines. People carry waxed cotton saddlebags. Ly-cra is banished to the lower layers. Out on the streets faux-couriers, dressed the part, cruise around on spotless steel track bikes, carrying enormous single-strap bags and wearing their bonsai cycling caps. But their bags are empty. They carry no radios. They wear the bottoms of their trousers rolled.

INTERVIEW

WITH

BEN LERNER

.

INSOFAR AS BEN LERNER'S NOVELS can be said to be 'about' anything, it might be argued that they concern the capacity of words to generate feeling: literature's tragic attempts to distil the felt intensities of lived experience into syntax, grammar; the blurring of fiction and personal history; consciousness on the street and on the page. But to paraphrase Lerner's own comments on the poetry of John Ashbery, made during our interview in London in early 2015, 'aboutness' is not what his novels are about. Though composed, or collaged, from real-world experiences – critics have made much of his novels as roman-à-clefs; sustenance for our reality-hungry times – both *LEAVING THE ATOCHA STATION* (2011) and *10:04* (2014) might more productively be thought of as experiences in themselves: books through which you move the way you move through a museum, or a week in your life. The journey's arc is less important than the diverse experiences it contains. The drugged languor that follows a trip to the dentist. A nervous break-down in the Prado. Seeing oneself from the outside, laughing in slow motion.

These moments – 'things that quicken the heart,' in the words of *10:04* – approach the epiphanic, though the veil is never quite lifted. Lerner is too smart, too self-aware for that: his books ironise the very notion that art can access transcendent truth. Discrete moments of af-fective intensity are typically the domain of poetry, and it was as a poet that Lerner began his career. He has thus far published three collections: *THE LICHTENBERG FIGURES* (2004); the National Book Award-nominated *ANGLE OF YAW* (2006); and *MEAN FREE PATH* (2010). His novels don't read like 'book-length poems', yet they continue his poems' investigation into the contaminated texture of contemporary language and thought.

Lerner's second and most recent novel, *10:04*, is by turns hilarious, frustrating, enlightened, enlightening, anxious, arrogant, provocative, and unaccountably (beautifully) sad. It concerns a year in the life of Ben, a Brooklyn-based writer who is, but is not, the author of the novel we hold in our hands. He receives a life-changing advance for his second novel. He eats, and then thinks about, octopi. He fretfully awaits large storms, cooks bland food for an Occupy protes-tor, watches cult films, ejaculates (with difficulty) into a cup. Most significantly, he listens, with varying degrees of concentration, as several people talk about their lives. Appropriately for a novel that disrupts the notion of linear time, thrusting the reader into an unstable space in which past and future, present awareness and distant memory, are in a constant state of negotiation, *10:04* is both a familiar and prophetic work. Addressing itself to the history of literature – to the ghosts of Robert Creeley and Walt Whitman, to the novel itself – it is equally, and more urgently, a message to the future. By assembling a book from the poems, photographs, anecdotes and experiences that already exist in the world, Lerner posits a strategy by which that world might be refreshed.

––––––––––

Q. THE WHITE REVIEW — *LEAVING THE ATOCHA STATION* features a description of Adam's approach to composition, in which he collages together a poem from scraps of mistranslated Lorca alongside lines from his diary. How accurately does that reflect your process as a writer? You include one of your own poems later in the book as if to corroborate the preceding account of how the poem was constructed.

A. BEN LERNER — Composition for me is pretty distinct in poetry and prose, although the commonality between them is that I never really know what I'm doing. You have to discover content in the exploration of the form. But with poetry I feel like I'm really listening to the language. I have a territory of concern, but it's the material life of the language, and the push and pull of it, that brings me into a form. And then when I start to find myself working in a particular structure – you know, if I find myself writing in tercets, or whatever – I make that a rule, I treat contingency as necessity. So it's this dialectic wherein I redescribe a chance operation as a restraint. In prose, with which I have less experience, I feel that I need to discover a prosody, a syntax that's alive with a kind of thinking. Both as a method of characterisation – I've written in the first person, so the prosody of the syntax is the rhythm of the character's thinking in time – and once I have some sense of that, then content takes care of itself. Patterns emerge, both on the level of the narrative and on the level of the language.

Q. THE WHITE REVIEW — In mainstream literary discourse the idea of the 'poetic' is pretty restrictive. It seems to boil down to some idea of euphony or lyricism, of an eloquence that elevates its subject. There are sentences in *10:04* that could be described as 'poetic',

but which are intentionally quite awkward at the level of syntax and word choice. Is that something that emerged from the need to find modes of expression that existed outside of the 'poetic', the 'lyrical' or the 'literary'?

A. BEN LERNER — Yeah. One example for me in *10:04* is the narrator's wilful reliance on a kind of inflated medical or technical vocabulary. I still want to control those sentences – they're still very much composed – but often what I'm trying to do is think about, not just the way that language can accurately measure experience, but its failure to take the measure of an experience. That matters in the book in lots of different ways. The narrator at one point describes himself as the number of his aortic diameter; he reduces moments of high sentiment, tears on his face, to 'lachrymal events'. It's kind of like the opening of *THE MAN WITHOUT QUALITIES*, Robert Musil's way of using this detached weather reportage. Part of its power is that you immediately feel the degree to which that discourse doesn't actually describe anything like the experience of the phenomenal world. Part of what you're doing in the heteroglot realm of the novel, or in poetry – in certain kinds of poetry, certainly the poetry I'm interested in – is thinking not just about the capacity of language to measure experience but dramatising the incommensurateness of certain vocabularies and certain experiences.

Q. THE WHITE REVIEW — That alienation can also be humorous. In *10:04* you use the phrase 'stout-bodied passerine' to describe a pigeon, for example. Later the narrator realises he has used the wrong term: misidentification as a form of slapstick.

A. BEN LERNER — It's intimately related to humour: the strategic disappointment of the expectations that a language creates. I think that

that's totally central to literary composition. The felt disconnect that humour acknowledges can also be the space for things like hope and critique. Those words are a little bit grand, but humorous moments are ones in which there's a revealing embodied response. Laughter is a physical response to the ill fit of the dominant fiction of the world, the dominant description of the world, and other moments of representation. Humour is a kind of a glitch or a tear in the matrix of the language that seems to me central to literature.

Q. THE WHITE REVIEW —— Humour in fiction can have a redeeming or recuperative quality, especially in the solemn context of literary fiction. At the same time, humour risks alienating or irritating the reader. Is the anxiety that humour can produce part of the modulation from irony to sincerity that you describe at the start of the novel?

A. BEN LERNER —— I wanted this book to start by acknowledging a ground in which sincerity would seem very difficult, and figure out a way to move towards a kind of un–ironic inhabitation of the pronouns – I mean avoiding 'irony' in the sense of ironic detachment. Irony is really important as a formal device. It's very intimately linked to humour: to say one thing but mean another. The self–reflexivity of the book and the way it refers to its own construction and procedures constitutes a really important part of its move towards sincerity. The book wants to acknowledge its own constructedness; it wants to think about the way that the fictions by which we live are themselves necessarily constructions. But I think that for a lot of people anything that smacks of self–reference is automatically some metafictional joke, a hall of mirrors or whatever. I'm not interested in that kind of metafiction.

Q. THE WHITE REVIEW —— These days the games that writers play are much more concerned with how their fictions relate to some notion of 'reality' or literal truth. In Alt Lit circles, for example, there's an assumption that social media allow for a kind of 'unmediated' mode of address that can circumvent the conventions of fiction, which is a strange position given that the internet *is* media.

A. BEN LERNER —— I'm totally comfortable with attacks on fiction. I think the problem is if it re–inscribes a new naiveté that says, for instance, 'the essay isn't constructed,' or that there's a kind of diaristic mode of writing that doesn't involve mediation. I think that one of the things that is maybe emphasised if your education is as a poet, or in the historical avant–garde, is that constructedness, which generally speaking is a bad thing for fiction writers, is a good thing for poets. The drama of construction and the way a form is put together, whether you call it fiction or non-fiction – there's an emphasis on mediation in poetry. Any writer who thinks that they can move from art to life in a way that makes the question of form disappear seems to me to be at best naïve.

Q. THE WHITE REVIEW —— Would you say that gesturing towards the constructedness of *10:04*, especially in terms of the content – the discussion of the writer's 'strong six–figure advance', the emphasis on the novel as a commodity form – express or align with a political position?

A. BEN LERNER —— One way to think about the politics of literature is the traditional avant–garde fantasy, which I'm sympathetic with but can't accept, where you want the poem to be a technology for actually changing history. There's also a kind of politically suspect fantasy where you want the book to be an imaginary solution to a real problem.

Q. THE WHITE REVIEW —— The utopian possibility of fiction?
A. BEN LERNER —— Worse than utopian. Fredric Jameson has talked about how certain works of literature want to resolve in the domain of the imagination contradictions that exist in reality, in order to prevent the resolution of contradictions in the world. You certainly don't want a book that's just an hour of escape from the regimentation of experience, just a compensatory fiction. But I do think that a book that tries to really acknowledge in as robust a form as possible the contradictions of its own making and its own moment can be a politically valuable work. Especially if it's trying to imagine spaces for thought and feeling that aren't totally circumscribed or foreclosed by the contemporary. One strategy to make a book overcome being merely a commodity – and a book is definitely a commodity – is to try to bring the material conditions of its own production into the domain of the fiction. I knew I wanted to go right at that stuff, even though people would find it off-putting.

Q. THE WHITE REVIEW —— People might find that stuff off-putting because it comes across as 'self-obsessed'.
A. BEN LERNER —— It's much less politically interesting to think that you can throw your voice, so to speak, and write as a 7-year-old Afghan girl or whatever, than it is to actually try to inhabit your present moment. The difference politically between my two novels is that LEAVING THE ATOCHA STATION is a kind of interrogation of solipsism. In *10:04* the narrator wants to experiment with a more Whitmanic emptying of himself, and to let all these other stories in. I don't think of the narrator of *10:04* as particularly interested in

himself, so much as trying to figure out modes of care and connection. Both narrators are concerned with the possibility of authenticity – the novel always has been. The alignment or misalignment of your internal experience with the outside world is what novels are made out of.

Q. THE WHITE REVIEW —— The idea of immanence – things being present without always being perceivable – is a theme in *10:04*. The book is laced with apocalyptic imagery, but the apocalypse never materialises; the storm fails to arrive twice. Collective proprioception is made present as a possibility, but that's all it ever amounts to. Where did this interest in immanence emerge from?
A. BEN LERNER —— I was really influenced by all these thinkers who were on the Left trying to think about totality, how capitalism invades every instant of our experience, and there's no outside. It's a traditional Left question for artists: how do you make art that can figure an outside to a murderous status quo if the materials you have at hand are so compromised? More recently I've been interested in those artists or thinkers who reject the notion of the totality of capitalism as too close to the neoliberal idea that capitalism has triumphed. And in fact there are moments in our life and in our experience which are not totally corrupt – they're not pure, but they're not totally corrupt. Immanence is a way of thinking about how redemption – however you want to conceive it – is always immanent with an 'a', even if you don't feel like it's imminent with an 'i'. If we're not going to simply despair, we have to be alive to the possibilities of the present. And maybe one thing art can do is seize and make shareable some of those moments.

Q. THE WHITE REVIEW —— Novels that dodge

politics entirely seem redundant to me; at the same time, I don't have any illusions that a book is going to change the world. There's a dialectic of needing to position oneself as a writer while at the same time being aware of the failure of political literature – especially within the novel, which has such a bourgeois history – having any measurable effect on the world. That negotiation can be productive, but it can also crush you.

A. BEN LERNER —— Totally. I feel like you can sometimes have useful debates about how one kind of literature will have more or less of a political effect, but I don't think that making literature is a way of making revolution. It's amazing how persistent that avant–garde fantasy has been. There's a moment in LEAVING THE ATOCHA STATION when Adam is hearing this debate about the avant–garde, and half making it up because he doesn't understand the Spanish. He says that he can't imagine literature, his poems, making anything happen. He can't imagine them stopping the war in Iraq. He can't even imagine them interfering in the smooth functioning of capital, let alone being a tactic of revolution. But when he tries to imagine a world without even the sorry excuses for poems that exist, he sees total despair. That's a negative way of saying, 'Well, art can both be ineffectual and totally crucial.' It's insisting on the importance of a domain of experience that isn't totally instrumentalised and militarised and commercialised, and that involves all kinds of privilege and contradiction, but that is still important.

Q. THE WHITE REVIEW —— This question is made concrete through the exploration of modes of address and interpersonal pronouns; the moments in 10:04 when you address the reader directly, for example. Who is the 'you'

to which these statements are addressed?

A. BEN LERNER —— It's a complicated question. I don't think I have an answer to it. These are the questions the book wants to pose: what are the possibilities figured by certain kinds of pronouns; what are the sites where the personal can become transpersonal; what are the modes of address that are available to art? There's a shift to a certain degree in my relation to pronouns where I'm trying to imagine contemporary reception. I don't mean the NEW YORK TIMES BOOK REVIEW. I mean 'contemporary reception' as in you and I existing at the same time. A lot of modernist, on the one hand, and Whitmanic literature, on the other, imagines itself as addressed to the future. In 10:04 I want to think about a coeval readership too – you are reading this right now – a kind of acknowledgement of the weird way that a book can be both a technology of time travel, and a way to feel hailed or excluded or participated with in the present moment.

Q. THE WHITE REVIEW —— That's figured in the book in lots of different ways. There are the moments of direct address; there are also the photographs, which in a sense are doing the same thing.

A. BEN LERNER —— Absolutely. The photographs in the book in part are ways of trying to think about looking together, where the looking in the narrative, and the looking of the reader, can become briefly coeval or correspond.

Q. THE WHITE REVIEW —— The grammar explored in 10:04 has a world–building quality. If you can figure out how two individuals can connect at the level of pronouns and interpersonal address, then that might become the atomic unit, as it were, for building larger social structures. This relates the figure of the octopus and the theme of proprioception – the flickering awareness of a larger social body.

A. BEN LERNER — Those are the metaphorics of the book. The distribution of the octopus's neurons at the cost of proprioception is both the figure for the dissolution of the self, and a different kind of self that could be collectivised or spread out. The book is concerned with showing the degree to which proprioceptions are fictions that are subject to re–description. You see yourself in the current of time, that is, in a narrative, but that self–image can in fact be re–described. When that happens, it's vertiginous and can be horrible, but it's also a moment of possibility.

Q. THE WHITE REVIEW — There's a strikingly vertiginous image in LEAVING THE ATOCHA STATION. Adam imagines looking directly upwards and seeing another version of himself looking down on him.

A. BEN LERNER — That's a bad circuit of solipsism, in a way. In 10:04 I want to think about how a similar doubling of vantages can be an opportunity to think about a more collective subjectivity, and to create a sense that the present is shot through with fictions about the past and the future, and they're up for grabs. I like what David Graeber has been saying recently against the notion of capitalism as a totality. He, among many others, has been emphasising how neoliberal capitalism in many ways has been revealed as an economic failure. We don't believe that it brings everyone up to the same level. We know it depends upon the immiseration of huge parts of the population. We know that growth is unsustainable ecolog–ically. But nobody seems to believe that there's any other way to do it. Graeber's point is that neoliberal capitalism is a total failure as an economic policy, and a total triumph as an ideo–logy. 10:04 is looking at these narratives that seem inevitable, but are fallible and shifting.

Q. THE WHITE REVIEW — There is an underlying sense in 10:04 of attempting to figure out to what degree a writer can claim to be engaged in the world in an active sense. Is that something that impinges on the politics of the novel?

A. BEN LERNER — Many of the artists that I really care about are incredibly engaged, or find a mode of engagement in a disengagement from certain dominant regimes of knowledge and information that's so thorough that it models different ways of thinking and feeling, if that makes sense. John Berger for me is both of those at once. He's an amazing thinker about technology, a pioneer of television, and really aware and engaged in all kinds of ways.

Q. THE WHITE REVIEW — Was Berger's work an inspiration for 10:04? He's a very intense man. I saw him read a short story for a Palestinian literary festival, and by the end of the story he was in floods of tears.

A. BEN LERNER — The way that Berger influ–enced me was more in his art criticism. For Berger, materialism – an attention to mate–rial contradiction – doesn't mean getting rid of sensuality, pleasure and lyricism. It means precisely attending to those things on ev–ery level, from the hummingbird to the war machine. I really admired that as a way of thinking about what art does. Being a ma–terialist doesn't just mean renouncing every available pleasure or feeling as 'bourgeois': it means being alive to the way that contradic–tions are lived. He did that so beautifully in his art criticism. For example his essay on Turner, where he talks about how Turner grew up in a barbershop – Berger says, in a throw–away line, that Turner would have seen a lot of blood and water and suds, and thinks about that in relation to the seascapes. It's an in–credible observation of painting and mundane

experience, and it's all about class and occupa-
tion. I really admire the way that he gets at
these little dialectical images. Have you read
his Booker acceptance speech? It's a badass
moment. *G.* is certainly about a kind of insis-
tence on the libidinal as a part of the political.
That's his thing. That's always been his thing.
10:04 talks about these energies that may be
fallen, the feeling you get when you have an
experience of the lubricity of the city, or some
kind of physical desire – those energies have
to be acknowledged as real. Berger stands for
that idea that a critical art, an engaged art, isn't
just about revealing every available aspect of
the present to be bankrupt; it's about really
embracing the sensual richness of the world,
no matter how fallen.

Q THE WHITE REVIEW — Do you think of your
work in relation to feminist writing? The work
of Chris Kraus, for example, incorporates art
criticism, politics, erotics, and autobiography.
It touches on that sensual richness you describe in Berger's writing and arguably goes
much further in its evocation of its abjection,
impulse and desire. The idea of a form of
art-oriented criticism filtered through the sub-
jective, desiring self strikes me as a feminist
position.
A. BEN LERNER — Totally. There's also a
hugely sexist reception that allows men to talk
about their experience and it's great literature,
but if you're Chris Kraus and you do it you
can be dismissed as an exhibitionist. It's really
fucked up. I admire Chris Kraus's work but
I don't know it so well. Eileen Myles and
Maggie Nelson are two contemporary writers
who I knew as poets first, but I really admire
their use of lived experience and also their
acknowledgement of how lived experience gets
transposed into literature, and literature itself
becomes lived, and both of their thinking about

art. I think of them definitely as company, and
as significant. I also think of my mom – she's a
feminist psychologist. My first novel involves
this kind of boy who is testing out the death
of his mom and has this huge anxiety about
presenting himself to these women. *LEAVING
THE ATOCHA STATION* was heavily influenced
by feminism, but instead of being a kind of
direct feminist proclamation, it's more about
thinking through a certain male psychology.

Q THE WHITE REVIEW — I wonder if the fallen
experience you spoke of earlier in relation to
Berger's criticism is an antidote to the 'profound
experience of art' that you satirise in *LEAVING
THE ATOCHA STATION*?
A. BEN LERNER — The closest thing to a
'profound experience of art' being achieved in
that book is Adam's reading of John Ashbery.
In a way 'art that changed my life' is an
apocalyptic rhetoric, right? Adam's reading of
Ashbery is more like, 'Oh it's this world but
a little different, briefly.' I think of Ashbery
as a great artist of the anti-apocalyptic. The
American critic and poet Chris Nealon wrote
this really beautiful essay about Ashbery and
'optional apocalypse' where he talks about
how, in Ashbery, there's always this freedom
to wander away from history, even while you
acknowledge it. Ashbery's been attacked for
that – the L=A=N=G=U=A=G=E poets were
always pissed off that he didn't take a more
political stance. But Ashbery's position, which
isn't a position that Berger would agree with,
is that art is art, and politics is politics, but all
art, if it's real art, is on the side of life. You
protect that in part by not making your art
programmatic.

Q THE WHITE REVIEW — Ashbery is a huge
presence in *LEAVING THE ATOCHA STATION*.
Did he shape your early poetry?

A. BEN LERNER —— Some poets I would read and think, 'Oh, this is incredible.' Or, 'Oh, this is horrible.' But with Ashbery I was like, 'What the fuck is going on? This thing *looks* like a poem...' I was in high school, reading him in Topeka. I remember I found a copy of his poems in Barnes & Noble, and I knew he was famous – he'd won all these prizes, right? I remember thinking, 'What is this thing?' I'm reading a poem and I feel like I know what's happening; I'm being taken along and it feels really beautiful, or really stupid all of a sudden; and then I look up and it all vanishes. There was this Ashberian sublime and the discovery moved and confused me profoundly.

Q. THE WHITE REVIEW —— Were you writing poems at that time?
A. BEN LERNER —— Yeah. I was writing some really bad poems.

Q. THE WHITE REVIEW —— Did you ever consider writing fiction before poetry?
A. BEN LERNER —— It was always poetry. At no point in my life did I attempt to write a single sentence of something I thought of as fiction. That's kind of still the case. There were works of fiction I loved, but they never made me want to write; or if they made me want to write, they never made me want to write fiction. I never read THE BROTHERS KARAMAZOV and was like, 'Okay, I think I can do this.' I didn't really have a sense of what my own relation to the novel would be. In a way I still feel like the best and worst thing about poetry – and maybe all writing, but especially poetry – is that you actually never get beyond that first moment of feeling like you're going to fake being a poet. It's still that, for me. What a fucking weird art! Having written a poem in no way guarantees that you can write another poem. In American writing programmes everyone talks about the

'craft' of writing. Cabinetmakers or carpenters can learn a stable set of skills, and if you've been called in to make a table five thousand times you're probably going to be really good at making tables, you can count on being able to do the job. But if you said to me, 'Write a poem right now,' I don't have that set of skills. It's this really weird thing where you commit to something as a lifelong practice that also feels impossible.

Q. THE WHITE REVIEW —— Can you still write poetry while in the middle of writing a novel? Do you ever start a poem and think it would work better as fiction, or vice versa?
A. BEN LERNER —— Sometimes they work in parallel; sometimes one takes over. I thought I was working on a book of poems when I wrote the poem that ends up being in *10:04*, and then this other frame grew around it. What I love about the novel is its elasticity, and its ability to assimilate other genres. When I'm writing a novel I feel like it can gather things that weren't originally conceived of as part of that novel. I wrote three books of poetry that were very much organised by book–length forms and rules, and the negotiation of the rule, and I decided after my third book of poetry that I wanted to write discrete poems. I didn't want the rule to be a macrostructure: I wanted to see what would happen when I wasn't doing that. One thing that happened as soon as I didn't have a book–length restraint was I wrote a novel.

Q. THE WHITE REVIEW —— You say you hadn't written a line of fiction up until that point. Do you remember the moment when you realised you were writing fiction? Was it a sudden shift, or something that emerged gradually?
A. BEN LERNER —— I'd written prose poems. I thought of the opening scene in LEAVING THE

ATOCHA STATION, which is set in the museum, as a narrative prose poem, but then I realised that there was a rhythm of thinking that wasn't satisfied with that little narrative. The prose poem ends with Adam leaving the museum – but what if I follow him out? Then what happens? All these ideas I'd had about poetics or art begin to take over, to insert themselves into his life in unpredictable ways. That thing that Tolstoy talked about – rushing home to see what Vronsky is going to do next – is true. Once you have a narrator who is moving through any kind of space, then writing becomes a little bit like the rudimentary video games of my youth. If you choose to go left, what's the new screen? What are the possibilities of movement or encounter? Well into that novel, I was still trying to maintain the fiction that I wasn't writing a novel.

Q. THE WHITE REVIEW —— 10:04 is filled with found objects or readymades – photographs, poems and short stories written before the novel itself. Is that porousness reflected in your strategies as a writer? Do you need to silence the world when you write?

A. BEN LERNER —— I need a weird mix of distraction and silence. Silence is too silent; total distraction is another thing. I can't write offline. I always want to see something, or Google a phrase. You get this real–time image of its place in the lexicon, in terms of hits. I'm writing this little monograph now on the hatred of poetry, why people denounce and defend poetry historically. You can Google 'I hate poetry' and test it against 'I hate piano' or whatever. It's funny. I'm always collaging. It's like what Bakhtin said about the novel, that the form is a celebration of heteroglossia, all these different languages within the language. The internet is this incredible heteroglot space. I want to see, like, 'Well, how does a physicist

talk again?' And there you have your physics paper. How did they talk in 1830? You go on Google Books. How do high school kids talk about physics? It's this incredible living image of speech and writing, and I steal from it all the time. I steal language from it all the time.

Q. THE WHITE REVIEW —— I found a Susan Stewart interview online. She's talking about futurity; the relationship between temporality and grammar. She writes: 'Despite its roots in prophecy, lyric throughout its long history has rarely been written in the future tense or concerned with the future as a theme. Even so, perhaps this persistent absence indicates something deeper about the free practice of lyric; this very openness may indicate that futurity is nowhere in lyric deixis because it is everywhere.'

A. BEN LERNER —— Lyric time is a really interesting concept. It's a big question. Susan Stewart is a really good thinker about the lyric. Do you know that book by Sharon Cameron, LYRIC TIME? The eternalised present of a certain kind of traditional lyric is very much about the future, but it's about the persistence of an idealised moment of speech. I can find that really beautiful or really off–putting. But I also think about this other lyric impulse, which is not about the preservation of a moment of the past into the future: it's really about a technology of time travel. It's like Keats' living hand: 'I hold it towards you.' Or it's Whitman's attempt to collectivise that experience: I'm ahead somewhere waiting for you; I've projected myself into the future; I'm looking over your shoulder as you read. For me, the miracle of textual time is not the way that you preserve the present tense of your moment as a writer, but the way that there's a renewable present tense of reading. That's what's so amazing about Ashbery. Whenever you pick up one of the great Ashbery poems and you're reading it, the poem comes alive. The poem is not an idealised description of the past and the traditional romantic notion of preservation. It's a machine for making the present tense of reading felt.

Q. THE WHITE REVIEW —— What you said earlier, about that moment when you looked up from Ashbery's poems and they were gone – I don't really get Ashbery, personally. I enjoy reading his poems, but I couldn't begin to tell you what they are 'about'.

A. BEN LERNER —— Aboutness is not what they're about. But in a funny way 'Self-Portrait in a Convex Mirror', his most conven-tionally celebrated poem, is about something: his poetics. It's very much about the way that works of art function in time, or age, or manage to defeat ageing, and manage to be present. Ashbery and Whitman are very different, but very similarly concerned with how to make pronouns present in the act of reading, so the 'I' and the 'you' aren't just from the past, but inhabitable positions in the renewable present of reading. It's about the poem as a technology for defeating time, because it's never just the moment it was in the past, it's available for experience in any number of presents.

PATRICK LANGLEY, JANUARY 2015

NEWSPAPER

BY

EDOUARD LEVÉ

(*tr.* JAN STEYN AND CAITE DOLAN-LEACH)

INTERNATIONAL

APPROXIMATELY TWENTY PEOPLE have died in a suicide bombing at a seaside resort hotel. A man carrying a backpack filled with explosives entered the hotel lobby and detonated the bomb in the middle of a group of people who had gathered in preparation for a walking tour. The majority of the victims were tourists, but their identities and their exact number could not be determined. The violence of the detonation has prevented forensic specialists from precisely reconstructing the bodies.

THE EXPLOSION OF A MOPED loaded with ten kilogrammes of dynamite in a busy neighbourhood has killed four police officers and a young girl of five. Public officials immediately attributed the bombing to a group of guerrillas. Two other bombs within the capital city were later defused. The guerrilla organisation and the government have now agreed to schedule a meeting to make a ceasefire agreement. This agreement, reached through the intervention of an international non-governmental organisation, has been accompanied by an increase in guerrilla bombings, especially of electrical pylons in the outskirts of the capital city.

FOUR POLICE OFFICERS have been killed and twenty people have been wounded in an attack on a foreign country's cultural centre. No organisation has claimed responsibility for the attack, which was perpetrated by four men on two motorcycles. The men used assault rifles to open fire on police officers changing sentry duty shifts. The assailants managed to escape. Since this wave of attacks, security has been considerably heightened for all this foreign country's official buildings. As the national holiday approaches, police have increased the number of checkpoints. The foreign country's minister of the interior asserts that this attack is the work of extreme-Left factions who are very active in the east of the country.

THE POLICE CLAIM TO HAVE ARRESTED six men who are believed to have ties with a terrorist network. Telephonic surveillance had revealed a plan to assassinate the president. One of these men was arrested upon disembarking an aircraft, but the police, having insufficient evidence to detain him, released him the following evening. The five other suspects were arrested in a garage that served as their place of worship. The police have confiscated videotapes, diaries and maps of various embassies.

FOUR MEN IN POSSESSION of industrial quantities of cyanide and maps of various embassies throughout the capital have been arrested. In the course of the raid, the police found a map of the city's water distribution network.

THE CYCLE OF VIOLENCE between two countries continues. A soldier from one of the two sides, wounded a few days ago, has succumbed to his injuries. The military from the same side has conducted forays into areas where enemy refugees are currently taking shelter. Many have been killed, including a leader of the rebel troops.

FOLLOWING A WAVE OF DEADLY ATTACKS, the government has elected to entrust the construction of a new spy ship to a multinational defence contractor. With a hull made overseas, this new ship, crewed by thirty sailors and eighty surveillance and code–breaking experts, will weigh three thousand tons and will afford the military important naval resources in gathering electronic intelligence.

OVER THE PAST TWENTY YEARS, the ruling president of a former colony has become the bloody dictator of a failed nation. The economic and agricultural infrastructure has been destroyed, and famine has struck hard. One citizen in two is unemployed, and one in four is HIV positive. Public services are non–existent, the judicial system is corrupt, the media state–controlled. Investors, teachers, and doctors have fled. The collapse of the country can be attributed to the dictator–president's obsession with power. He refuses to tolerate any opposition and denies his constituents the right to vote. 'The opposition, if there is any, will never govern, not while I'm living and not after I'm dead. My ghost will come back to haunt them. They will be harassed by goblins and witches. I have a degree in violence,' he has said. His terrorising method relies on intimidation, as well as the removal (or more accurately, the murder) of his adversaries. Electoral fraud, false official statements, false accusations, and arbitrary arrests are the norm. The executors of these sinister acts are typically unemployed men, who are paid by the day, or gangsters, recruited from bars. The 'enemies' are the former colonisers and the ethnic minority living in the country. Wealthy farmers are targeted and their lands are redistributed to the dictator and his cronies. In the past ten years, agricultural production has been cut by half. Despite warnings from regional leaders that these practices risk ruining the country by causing foreign capital to flee, the administration has relentlessly hunted down former colonialists. Nor has the dictator neglected to punish the ethnic minority; he has formed a special group, the so–called 'sixth brigade,' composed of former officers from a foreign country, who distinguished themselves there by committing full–scale genocide. The atrocities proliferate: villagers burned alive, infants skewered on their mother's backs, families forced to sing songs on the graves of their loved ones. One of the sixth brigade's customs is to ask their victims: 'Long sleeve or short sleeve?' – a question intended to determine whether the victims prefer to have their whole arm or just their hand amputated.

F

A SMALL MUNICIPALITY is scheduled to open a centre for the study and archive of the dictatorship that made this village its temporary headquarters during the
last war. Initially, the museum honouring this dictator was intended to be open to the
public. But now, following pressure from former resistance fighters, the archive is
intended to function as a university research centre, with restricted access to its documents. The archival centre relies on two sources of funding, one belonging to a former
defence minister of the totalitarian regime in question, the other stemming from a call
to the public to assist in the project's completion. The former dictator is coming back
into style. The municipality, in agreement with the hotel owner's union, is promoting
this image, hoping that this 'fashionable' dictator will attract tourists to the area. The
leader's former residence, which was commandeered from a rich family whose son
committed suicide rather than collaborate with the regime, has been transformed into
a five-star hotel wherein delighted tourists pay the equivalent of one month's salary
to spend one night in the 'big man's' bedroom suite. The national poet responsible for
writing all of the dictator's speeches lived nearby; his former château welcomes two
hundred thousand visitors each year. The tour continues onward to the living quarters
of the militia's generals, to the residence of the Black Shirts' commanding officers, past
the headquarters of the Always More division, a branch of the commando unit which
specialised in cruelty, and lastly, visits the home of a 'model citizen,' who massacred
countless members of his own religious order by deporting them to a bordering nation, where they were industrially exterminated. An official tourist guide says, 'The
true history of the city remains to be discovered. We hope that the study centre will
help with this task.'

IN A BLACK BRIEFCASE, a former dictator carries the documents that will
enable him to respond to accusations levelled against him. Three weeks after the
proceedings at the international tribunal have kicked off, he is less interested in def-
ending himself than in preparing his image for posterity. Rather than addressing
himself to the victims, judges, or to global opinion, he looks to his comrades to offer
him a sort of rehabilitation, in spite of the fact that it is they who have offered him up
to the international justice system. The former dictator remains calmly seated while
witnesses, all of whom are victims of ethnic cleansing, describe crimes and civilian
deportations. He asks them questions, hoping to intimidate. Then, from out of his
briefcase, he takes statements from opposing witnesses to prove that international
security forces and another ethnic group's military are responsible for these atrocities.
His strategy has paid off: a recent survey has shown that half of his nation's population finds his testimony convincing. He is taking advantage of the ruling classes' fear
of the international tribunal. Some of them have remained in power after his dictatorship. When a man belonging to the victim ethnicity states that two of his children

were killed on his doorstep by the ex-dictator's police force, which had come to his home not in order to flush out weapons belonging to 'terrorists' but rather to kill men, pregnant women and children, the former leader merely responds: 'You both belong to the same ethnicity. Otherwise he would have killed you.'

IN A SMALL COUNTRY recently on the receiving end of a superpower's retaliatory air raids, an earthquake has caused approximately fifty deaths. A global humanitarian programme has reported one hundred people missing. The superpower has continued its air strikes in the east of this small country, where rebel fighters can still be found. Over five thousand soldiers are involved in the operation.

AN OUTBREAK OF THE PNEUMONIC PLAGUE has caused four deaths in the south of the country. After having distributed antibiotics to seventeen thousand people, health authorities are claiming that the epidemic is probably contained.

TWO HUNDRED HAVE DIED following a fire on a packed train.

A YOUNG, 24-YEAR-OLD WOMAN has wed the king. Born to a modest family, she lost her mother at the age of 3. When her father remarried, she was sent to live with her grandmother, where she grew up an only child. She is well educated, having attended a technical institute where she majored in management systems and decision theory. Beautiful and intelligent, she was discovered while working at one of the king's business interests, where a member of the king's entourage noticed her. The king, still single at the age of 38, asked to meet her over dinner, and the marriage was announced several weeks later. Getting married is the perfect act of faith. What would otherwise have been a simple political event has become a real-life fairy tale. 'Our king is a social monarch,' one commentator has said.

SOCIETY

OVER THE COURSE OF A LIFETIME, one woman in every five becomes a victim of domestic violence. The likelihood of women aged 15–45 being wounded or killed because of domestic violence is greater than the combined likelihood of their becoming victims of cancer, malaria, traffic accidents, or war. Every week, several women die as a result of spousal abuse, which is the cause of 50 per cent of divorces. This violence takes an economic toll in the form of raised healthcare costs. Only 10 per cent of women press charges. The assailant's personality profile is that of a jealous, alcoholic man with inconsistent income, little self-esteem and a childhood history of violence. For years, media images of battered women have alerted the public to the problem. One woman is burned alive by her husband. Another disfigured woman makes the headlines of a weekly paper under the title, 'The Savage Family'. A third woman, concealed behind a scarf, denounces her husband on television, explaining that she has already pressed charges against him seventeen times, without result. After the show is broadcast, the husband stabs her and punctures her lung. The number of victims has, however, remained more or less constant for decades.

THE ARMY IS PUTTING TOGETHER A MANUAL for urban warfare, intended for its troops. Cities have become battlegrounds, where attempts are being made to both contain rowdy crowds and attack enemy forces. The urban setting is a theatre of operations in its own right, but its particular configuration requires specific training, which, up until now, has been ignored by the default training programme. Traditional combat in rural areas has given way to engagements on the ground (streets and buildings), underground (the subway, sewers, parking lots, tunnels), and in above-ground structures (bridges and streets). This labyrinthine, unruly environment requires specific precautions and has necessitated the creation of new training grounds, where fragments of cities, rather than traditional villages, have been artificially reproduced.

A STUDY HAS REVEALED that 57 per cent of skiers ignore trail markers.

A RESIDENTS' ASSOCIATION is filing a complaint against X, regarding groups of young people who congregate in the streets on the weekend to imbibe alcohol together. They buy bottles at the supermarket and assemble in the street until dawn, getting drunk with friends or with strangers. They don't have the means to buy similar quantities of alcohol in bars. The crowds can contain several hundred individuals. These mobs are noisy and last until morning, leaving behind empty bottles and traces of vomit. The drinkers are typically between the ages of 13 and 20.

A FAMOUS WRITER has been sentenced to a fine of ten thousand monetary units by the court. This fine follows a guilty ruling in a defamation suit brought by the family of a woman who was savagely murdered. The writer had written a book in which he strongly defended the alleged murderer.

LAST YEAR, A FAMOUS ACTOR was found guilty of using 'abusive language and intimidation' toward a flight attendant. This year, he was prosecuted for purchasing heroin. The latter charges were subsequently dropped.

F

OTHER NEWS

TWO YOUNG PEOPLE, ages 16 and 18, are being investigated for the rape and murder of a sixty–nine–year old grandmother; the 18–year–old, a legal adult, is being charged with aggravated murder and aggravated rape, with accompanying acts of torture and abuse, while the 16–year–old is being held as an accomplice. Both have been arrested and detained in custody. One of the victim's friends called the police after finding the elderly woman dead in the living room, savagely beaten, covered in blood, and with a cracked skull. The woman, a former nursing assistant, mother of five, grandmother, and great–grandmother, spent her days lighting up the rooms of local nursing homes, regaling residents with her interpretations of oldie–but–goodie songs. The autopsy revealed that the victim had been raped using a microphone, which was most likely acquired at the scene. She suffered in agony for several hours before dying of internal bleeding. An initial witness, a man in his seventies, who is an amateur opera singer as well as the victim's neighbour, was being held in custody, but was cleared of any wrongdoing through DNA evidence, which indicated that there were several attackers. Eventually, after the neighbourhood's residents came forward with information, the police arrested a 16–year–old man who lived next door to the victim. The young man, who is a minor, admitted to the crime and implicated another 18–year–old man. The pair was apparently convinced that the woman was hiding a large sum of money in her home. The house had been torn apart in a search, but nothing was stolen; the two young men stated that they hadn't intended to kill her. The police were stunned by the young men's composure during questioning, but are sceptical, as the boys' self–portrayal as mere juvenile delinquents doesn't correspond with the savagery of the murder. Neither boy has a criminal record, but they are both well–known by the police. The older boy was arrested for violent robbery in front of a middle school, and the younger was questioned for fencing stolen goods, and later for burglary.

A PASTOR HAS BEEN SENTENCED to life in prison for the murder of six of his family members. His daughter, who participated in five of the six murders, was awarded a ruling of extenuating circumstances, and was sentenced to only twenty–one years in prison. She herself fired the shots that killed her mother and brother. Raped by her father for years, she became pregnant several times. He forced her to destroy the foetuses in a solution of toilet–cleaner; the same method was used to dispose of the family's bodies. The pastor has denied the accusations, stating that 'it's not up to me to prove that my family members are still alive. It's up to the justice system to prove that they're dead.' Only one of his children survived, another daughter, with whom he had a son; paternity has been confirmed with DNA testing. Faced with this new evidence, the accused responded: 'My daughter stole my sperm, she captured it in a condom. She used to sleep in the conjugal bed, and would wipe herself with the towel my wife used after we had sex. The expert who did the analysis is young; he has a lot to learn.'

THE SWOLLEN BODY of a 25-year-old woman has been found in an underground parking garage, located beneath a building. According to initial evidence, the death seems to be the result of a love affair gone wrong.

BUSINESS

A FOCUS GROUP of industry leaders has published its *PROPOSALS FOR THE SUCCESSFUL NATION: CONVERSATION AND CHANGE*. While the group has been careful to keep its distance from right-wing politics, the report is nonetheless in accordance with the conservative defence of a free economy. The group calls for a lighter and simpler tax system, a reduction in inheritance taxes and the abolition of taxes on investments and employers that it believes may stifle the economy. As regards employment, the organisation suggests increased flexibility in applying workweek limitations. 'Everyone should have the right to work as much as they want,' the document states. The group also declared itself in favour of establishing minimum service requirements during strikes, saying, 'We have to guarantee everyone the right to work.' Similarly, on the retirement age, they claim that 'employees should be able to work for as long as they choose.' State pensions, which have been endangered by an ageing population, should be substituted with a free-market solution. The so-called 'reign of bureaucracy,' which 'has become more attractive than employment in the private sector', must be looked into. According to the group, the government must withdraw from public enterprise and must introduce free competition into markets where 'monopolies are causing damaging delays in this time of increasing globalisation.' This disinvestment will allow for the reabsorption of public debt, which must be reduced to less than half of GDP.

FOR THE FIRST TIME EVER, the electronics industry is seeing a negative growth rate. The decline in the video market has not been compensated for by the sale of DVDs, and the sale of audio equipment is experiencing a downturn. Apparently, the uncertainties created by digital convergence have not encouraged consumers to open their wallets. Having announced the era of high-speed internet and wireless devices, larger brands are now refocusing on less complicated and more user-friendly appliances. Development plans for wireless, digital, and voice-command technologies in the home have been abandoned in favour of cheaper, hybrid products whose sole innovation is to combine multiple functions that were previously available only on separate devices. 'I think we're in a transitional period. In these fast-paced times, industries will refocus on their real strengths, with products that translate into cold, hard cash,' one analyst said. The technology sector is relying on the successful launch of new video-game consoles to reverse the downward trend.

'THE CURRENT INTEREST RATE will in no way inhibit the renewal of economic growth,' the president of the Central Bank has stated.

A COUNTRY HAS ANNOUNCED that it will be extending insurance coverage for airline companies in the event of war or terrorist attacks.

AN AIRLINE IS RECRUITING 'petite' stewardesses who are 'compatible with the size of the aircraft'. These new stewardesses are less than 1.60 metres tall while the average height in the industry is 1.70 metres. The company is claiming that, given that these planes have low ceilings, taller hostesses will experience stiff necks and lower back pain from trying to stand upright in the small space. 'If you've got someone a bit bigger, before long they'll experience injuries and discomfort, which can lead to disabilities that will permanently affect their work. This negatively impacts safety as well as profit,' said a spokesperson.

THE EMPLOYEES OF A LARGE RETAILER selling books, CDs, and electronics have gone on strike following the breakdown of salary negotiations with senior management. Workers were hoping to secure a salary increase after nine years of stagnant wages. Several stores in the capital city have been barricaded to prevent customers from entering, and union leaders are threatening to extend the strike to rural branches. Employees of a competing chain, as well as those of a perfume sales company, have supported the strike, coining the slogan, 'Down with global casualisation, down with casual globalisation.'

SCIENCE AND TECHNOLOGY

MANUFACTURERS OF AN EXPERIMENTAL Alzheimer's vaccine have announced their decision to suspend their first immunisation campaign to fight this degenerative neurological disease, which is currently incurable. The decision comes after multiple cases of meningitis appeared without explanation amongst patients who had been treated with the vaccine. A managing researcher stated, 'Investigations to understand this outbreak are presently underway.'

A DOZEN PEOPLE HAVE BEEN EXPOSED to radiation–contaminated gases
after a particle accelerator malfunctioned. According to the Department of Protection
against Ionising Radiation, the incident is not a serious one; a manager stated, 'The
exposure sustained is equal to that experienced during a full year by someone working in a factory.'

CLASSIFIEDS

FOR RENT: Furnished room for a single, employed man.

FOR RENT: Studio apartment bathed in light, with kitchen, bathroom, shower, fifth
floor, south–facing, clear view.

FOR SALE: Studio apartment, twenty–four square metres, five minutes from the
subway, on eighty square metres of green space. Garden, trees, downtown country-
side.

MUST SELL: Due to immediate relocation, selling two–bedroom balcony apartment, sixth floor, elevator, parking, great view. Urgent.

FOR RENT: Two–bedroom, 50–square–metre apartment in a gorgeous, large stone
building, sixth floor with elevator, no buildings opposite, south–facing.

FOR RENT: Two x three–room apartment in a beautiful renovated building, fifth
floor with elevator, star–shaped layout, exposed beams. Charming.

HIS SURVIVING WIFE, sons, daughters, and grandchildren are pained to announce a man's passing: the funeral services will be held in a private setting.

A CELEBRATED DOCTOR has passed away. He is survived by his wife, children, grandchildren, and great–grandchildren. He was awarded an honorary position
as department chief in a large hospital on his ninety–fourth birthday. The funeral will
be a religious ceremony held in his hometown's church.

A WOMAN HAS DEPARTED this world to find peace in the next. Her husband,
mother, children, brothers, sisters–in–law, and their families, and everyone who sur-

rounded her throughout her life, will gather together around her remains, to pray together for her eternal salvation.

WE ARE SEEKING a senior consultant, who will independently manage client relations, and who will, through compelling presentations, be an important partner for each and every client. Open to new approaches, the ideal candidate will be able to target new potential clients and be proactive. He or she will support the company's learning environment and participate in cross-departmental teams. He or she will be an enthusiastic leader and will contribute substantially to our business. The ideal candidate will have an advanced degree, and at least eight years of experience in consulting, prime contracting support, and leading complex projects.

WE ARE LOOKING FOR SOMEONE who is at ease with other people, has a taste for excellence, works well in teams, and has an entrepreneurial spirit, to join and grow with our company.

MOTIVATION: Because our 50,000 employees throughout the globe work within dynamic, independent, trustworthy teams. Pride: Because our business is a key figure in the industry, due to our innovative problem-solving strategies. Satisfaction: Because every employee participates in making our clients happy, regardless of their position.

IF YOU WANT TO CHANGE the direction of your life, we invite you to join one of our teams as a commercial engineer.

WEATHER

AIR DISTURBANCES ARE CIRCULATING in a rapidly moving front from the west/southwest. The northwest region is experiencing rain and winds. The high-pressure system over the south is protecting southern regions, where it is sunny.

SPORTS

WITH A RED FACE AND HOLLOW EYES, the player succumbs to the sun blazing over the stadium where the women's singles final is being held. She had four match points in her favour, but she finally gave in to her opponent, after a pitiless onslaught from the baseline that lasted over two hours (4–6, 7–6, 6–2). Yet for much of the game, having won the first set, at one point serving with a lead of four games to love in the second set, and later having four match points in the final game of the competition, the player looked like she was headed for her first international tournament win in the past four years. But each time, she yielded to her opponent. Her record now reflects seven losses in twelve finals. During the breaks, she put on a refrigerated cooling vest in an attempt to lower her core temperature, while her opponent opted for an ice pack on the back of her neck. Her rackets were kept in a large cooler in order to maintain the appropriate tension in their strings. The heat required the players to pause between games, sitting for just a few moments beneath the judge's umbrellas. During longer breaks, the players lay down. Their trainers covered their bodies in ice packs. Several spectators suffering from heatstroke were taken away in ambulances. The crowd, which favoured the opponent, was not immediately engaged, as long exchanges frequently ended in unforced errors. But the match's several unexpected twists ultimately thrilled the twenty thousand enthusiasts, including the player's mother, who was seated in the crowd sporting a white sunhat. After winning the tournament, the opponent raced over to her father, who was wearing a sunhat adorned with the colours of the national flag. The defeated player tried to cast her loss in a positive light, saying: 'I've just had two hard months following my ankle injury. But my performances at the start of this season have surpassed all my hopes.'

ARTS AND CULTURE

THE AUTHOR IS 45 YEARS OLD. After a dozen novels, two of which were truly successful (a prize for one, a cinematic adaptation for the other) he has released a collection of new short stories that range in tone between nostalgia, humour, despair, and utopia. In the collection we encounter, among other characters, the members of an exiled family who are seeking their roots on a remote island, a disenchanted lawyer who reveals to anyone who will listen the sordid family affairs that have unfurled in his office during his forty-year career, a rudderless lover roaming the public squares of the capital, and a retired couple who create a phalanstery for young men on a hill overlooking a commercial port. Short sentences, restrained emotion: using straight-forward, sober, efficient language, these short tales of lives lived paint a panoramic image of the difficulty of being together, and the impossibility of being alone.

IN THIS IMPRESSIVE BIOGRAPHY peopled with astonishing characters, we glimpse the future writer in the bright, redheaded child who was educated by two ultra-religious parents, and grew up into a sceptical young man. We also follow his brother, who emancipates himself, and his sister, who quietly withers away. The book

is above all worthwhile for its investigation of the country villages and city neigh‑
bourhoods that were home to the writer's family. There is virtually no remaining
trace of this family, nor of the millions of other victims of the genocide unleashed
upon their religious community.

A ROCK‑AND‑ROLL SINGER is selling the costume he wore during a legend‑
ary performance in an online auction. Proceeds will go to a charity fighting against
world hunger. The skin‑tight, sequined get‑up is 'symbolically signed on the heart',
the entertainer stated.

TEN YEARS AFTER THE SCANDAL provoked by his production of one of his
country's seminal dramatic works, a foreign director has stepped back into the lime‑
light with another of his fetishistic productions. He isn't planning a dress rehearsal.
He feels that the preparation is an endless process, a process that is more interest‑
ing than performances. 'Rehearsals are the goal of performance, not the other way
around,' he said. Actors rehearse without scenery, and are introduced to the set just
days before the premiere, in order to help them appear untarnished by spatial habits.
He selected for his cast seven actors and two actresses, all of whom work with the
national theatre. 'You are experienced actors, but your experience doesn't interest me,'
he is reported to have told them at the first cast meeting. An actress said of working
with him, 'I prepared myself for hard work. I said to myself: "We'll be turned inside
out, like gloves." We were, but not like I imagined. I thought, since he aims to turn
the human being inside out, the same would go for the actor. But he did the opposite.'
Another actor confirmed that 'with him, you fall back on to your expertise or take
comfort in the director's guidance. He knows where he wants to go, but he doesn't
show you the way to get there. It's up to us to find it.' The work is intense, the director
is demanding. He destroys habits learned through years of conservatory training, us‑
ing a method he developed over years working in his own country. Actors start their
day with a martial arts practice that helps regulate their breathing and directs sounds
through space; their bodies become the axis point between a vertical line formed
by their spinal column, and a horizontal line that connects their mouth to the back
of the theatre. They pronounce simple syllables, in order to think of themselves as
no longer human, but as pure sound. Then they settle into a circle with the director,
where he makes them recite fragments of the text out of order, having forbidden them
to memorise the script. 'Working face‑to‑face, we just realised one day that we knew
the script, without knowing why or how,' an actor commented. 'With this man, the re‑
hearsal space once again becomes sacred. We're outside of time. He asks philosophi‑
cal questions, he requires us to embody concepts. Obviously, this raises questions, and
the absence of an answer sometimes becomes a source of outrage. Further down the

line, the world will acknowledge what he has brought to theatre.'

A CHOREOGRAPHER HAS INTRODUCED a new work made up of multiple segments, each with its own rules, physical sets, audio accompaniment, and number of dancers. Independently produced over the course of an entire year, the segments have been rehearsed separately, in different venues, and then assembled just three weeks before the first performance. The production and performance team includes a song-writer, lighting engineer, set designer, and a dance company, whose dancers perform alone, in pairs, or in trios, according to which segment they are presenting.

ENTERTAINMENT GUIDE

MOVIES

IN PARALLEL UNIVERSES, we each have our own duplicates. As soon as one of them dies, its strength is absorbed by the surviving versions. An outlaw travels amongst these universes, killing his duplicates and seizing their power.

A YOUNG, 18-YEAR-OLD MAN grows up hard on the streets, surrounded by urban poverty. There, he discovers love and friendship. A brutal testimony of those living on the margins.

ABANDONED ON A DESERT ISLAND by a mysterious military force, school-children kill each other in an initiation rite mandated by the government.

A LITTLE HORSE SPOTS PIRATES near its village, but no one believes it. Frustrated, the animal decides to leave its home island, where no one takes it seriously, and strikes out to confront the villains alone.

EXHIBITIONS

A WRITER who is also a multi-faceted director was given free rein curating this exhibition, which displays works he selected from a museum of modern art.

TWO HUNDRED PHOTOGRAPHS by an artist and writer who crossed paths with the biggest stars of his time. Their portraits are displayed with elegance and nostalgia.

THE RECENT SCULPTURES of a 30-year-old artist; this is his first solo exhibition. Sequins on polystyrene shapes give the show a childish, nightclub vibe.

THEATRE

THE POWER OF WORDS and the force of the imagination create scents, images, and sounds, transporting the viewer to a heightened state of pleasure and discovery.

IN THIS WORK, the writer portrays a woman destined to become a vessel for the whole world's memories. It is an invitation to travel into the unconscious and the unsaid, where silences are as eloquent as words.

WHILE SUFFERING FROM AN INCURABLE DISEASE, a man receives a visit from his lifelong friend, an implacable old dandy. The room fills up with more and more zany visitors, whose laughter ultimately triumphs over the fear of death.

LUKE RUDOLF

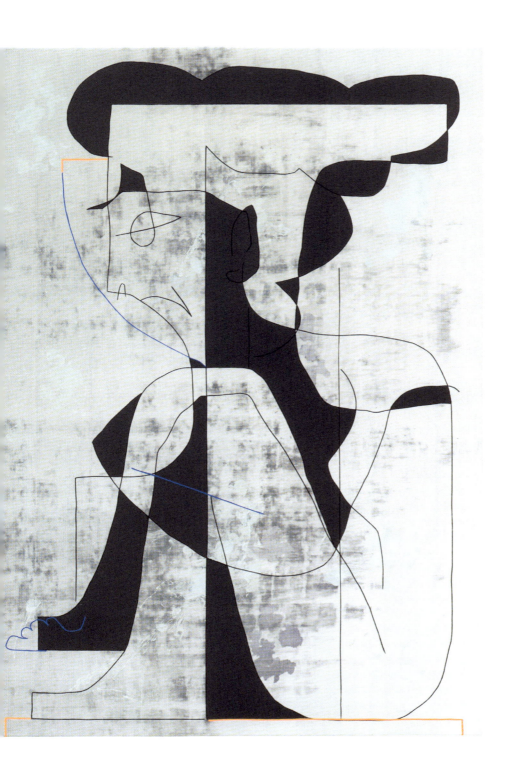

VI

VII

POEMS

BY

HOLLY PESTER

WATERMEN

It's Saturday and two men arrive at the door in the uniform. Thames Water.
We're checking the whole street, can we check your pipes. They walk through to

the back. Their boots are very large in the flat. A dog stretches her neck and smells
the air around the genitals. They are sorry. We are sorry but we have

some bad news. We have detected some contamination coming from one of the
addresses on this street and it's you. Your clean water and your waste pipes are

misconnected. Your waste pipe is going straight to The new river opened in 1613 to
bring fresh water from Hertfordshire to London. Don't worry it's not your

fault and we're not going to fine you. But it is illegal and you have to fix it. What it.
You're it. Your waste pipe. Your water pipe. Our waste. Our pipe. Your waste

pipe is misconnected and your cistern is flowing into the clean water of the New
River opened in 1613 to bring fresh water from Hertfordshire to London. There

are two types of sewer private and public. Private sewers belong to the customer. You.
You are responsible for the pipes that belong to you. There are

public sewers that belong to us the water company. We are the water company. Also
there are highway drains and gullies. And you know, swans. Are you related

to a plumber, No. Are you friends with one, No, Then you're going to have to hire one.
The men leave. I haven't been yet me neither you go. I didn't expect the

shame of ownership to be so closely related to the shame of having a body. (But it's not
mine none of it's mine) In 1946 the water supply to New River Head was

truncated at Stoke Newington with the New River ending at the East Reservoir. We
do customer shits straight into the West Reservoir Water Sports Centre is a

water sports and environmental education centre which is located in a picturesque
corner of leafy Stoke Newington. The centre provides the

opportunity to take part in sailing and kayaking for adults and children under the
watchful eye of expert instructors. The centre is operated by a charity social

enterprise we take our dog there there's swimming lessons. Your daily sewage
discharges direct to the new river. Did you know that it's neither new nor a

river. You just need to connect right, pipes. Good practice, good pipes. Do you have
relatives? If you need help you could contact the sewage network action

programme. SNAP. Would you like their number, No. The design and construction is
often attributed to Sir Hugh Myddleton. I walk my dog along the

new river path and do it properly doing good practice. I bag it and bin it. Any bin just
do it. She eats the swan shit. Nobody asked her to do that she just does it.

The new river path is not a public right of way but the owner allows access. The
owner is Thames Water. The shit bullies. SNAP. Let's go I need to go this morning

after coffee and think about strangers coming round. When I was little I came
downstairs to find police men in the living room a cat sniffing the air around

their genitals after there was a pub–fight. There was a piece of my college artwork on
the wall and I thought please don't let the police men look at the

pink print of my belly and leg. The man in the home wrote a poem about it, it was
about the difference between being at home and at work. It went when you are

at home you are not at work and when you are at work you are far from home but
sometimes men come into your home and they are at work. The relative

P

impurity of the new river is naught point nine. You're welcome for our contribution.
We live at number 55 point A. I do special direct transmission to

the swans and the geese and the one dead moore hen of the New River that opened in
1613 to bring fresh drinking water from the river gods to London.

JOKES THAT DON'T TRANSLATE

The man from Okay (Haitian – Traditional)

'how do you like it here?'
they asked him all wet animal
bites dust eye lashes trampoline
covers as coats
'We've come from the worst hit spot'
really staring as he fixed them
drinks It's OK 'OK?
We were hoping for more

         We've travelled such a way and we're hungry l
         ook at our cattle we're all present tense
       blistering tired disqualified deforged get it alien–like
              so tired'

OK put it
this way when I came here
I had nothing no language,
no clothes my body was limp
they took me in here fed me
here (points to neck and tum) made
me clothes here (points to chest) spoke
to me in Okay sang to me in Okay
danced at me to Okay vouched
for me swabbed me propagated
my value oracled my speed & fate
and the speed of my fate (strokes hair)
documented it all in Okay
'OK OK how long have you been here?'
I
was
born
here

Cock (French – Modern)

I took my dad to the shopping
the other day to buy new
shoes (he is 89)
we decided to eat cafeteria
noticed that ever a teenager
next to him
instead of hair he had red
crest – what a punk!
my father watched him closely
whenever teenager turned
he jisted my father and heard
him maybe chicken sound

Then teenager had enough

What happens old? You never
did crazy? Knowing my father
I swallowed not for choking on
the reply very relaxed without
blink he said you're beautiful

This old (Scottish – Heritage)

Olgirl was aafa crabbit
and bade by helsel
but for a cat
aa wey with her

uncivil andoo worth nothing really, bo?
you know
her dream lodge was
sum coast rent

drove well–straight a–crescendo
downed folk her cross
word finger & her finger finger
were the same finger

blathered in toon
boot bread an ecos
her back page is good
her back yard s heated

one day the Devil wit his act
and ellesse kit came til see her
'you know' he says 'youre wastin your time here'
'I know' she says

les bargin for one comprehensive
wish
'crack it to me, girl, fan your time comes
yill come to hell with me', bo?
No pause
'I want self–expression' she says
come to? he says
'I want to know myself' she says I want autonomy
for my hands to make sense

to only me sel so
only I can feel
myself For my fet and heed to
be ample reaching for one thought

and mood she says
My fat and my feelins
the same shesays my pets and my
admin inta meshed

my stoop to be concave the
rattle in my throat fused
to all other rattle sounds
like internet

And I want to be the champ–
ion of bullet music she says
rough and practical I'll
feed mysel on butcher grade philosophy

singularity of hairpins
sugar physics

the devil was dribbling adidas
 'I don't get it' he says
tell me
again, 'fine,
here's my project. I want yu ta make

dead. 'who?' The town – dead
(the
cath
e
dral?)
my old man ex–trah dead

P

thy sex dead all bodies ded &
differing & stinking yeah
the mayor – dummydallionstrangle

locals unanimalously deaded
it's   hap   pen   ing   now
it's nearly over
the nearly overly so feeding off their
deafers, a pearly deff one felt

gorily and fast, conservatoire pimps
down coocs, pops in is crate
I   t   s   h   a   p   p   e   n   i   n   g

sons of mark and nu reporters lay them inside

WRITERS FROM THE OLD DAYS

BY

ENRIQUE VILA–MATAS

(*tr.* J. S. TENNANT)

What else is there / other than knowing how to get off the ropes
—Mario Santiago

Augusto Monterroso wrote that sooner or later the Latin American writer faces three possible fates: exile, imprisonment or burial.

I met Roberto Bolaño right at the end of his period of imprisonment, although it would be more properly called one of anonymity, of isolation, being shut away.

I met him on 21 November 1999 at Bar Novo in Blanes, a kind of *granja catalana*, one of those places characterised by their spotless milk–churn decor, but in reality they're as foul as they are supposedly hygienic and all the more so for those who, like me in those days, loved the murky darkness of big nocturnal bars.

I'd gone into the Novo with Paula de Parma to have a juice, and I'd just ordered it when Bolaño walked in. Paula, who used to work at a secondary school in Blanes, had just read *DISTANT STAR* (recently published by Anagrama) and I remember like it was yesterday her asking Bolaño if he was Bolaño. He was, he said. And I, Bolaño added, was Vila–Matas...

'Holy Fuck!' we heard uttered soon after.

The exclamation was Bolaño's, and I have the impression the following conversation lasted as long as 'the drawn out laughter of all these years', as Fogwill would say.

I remember that I always talked to Roberto like we'd known each other all our lives. He was living with his wife Carolina López and their son Lautaro at 17, Carrer del Lloro (Parrot Street), and kept a little work space at no. 21. At no. 19 was the butcher's where he got the inspiration for the memorable poem 'Among Flies': 'Trojan poets / Now that nothing that might have been yours / Exists / Neither temples nor gardens / Nor poetry / You're free / Admirable Trojan poets'.

He didn't have a telephone and his post box was at no. 441, where he'd hear if he'd picked up some regional prize; the most recent of these was from San Sebastián at the end of 1996 for the story 'Sensini', a masterpiece. The value of that prize was really a very modest amount but Carolina and Roberto, who were living off her state salary, received the news with an enthusiasm more fitting for the Nobel than for a local competition.

My none too eloquent personal journal – composed with a certain dryness, containing just dates, notes and short comments – is, however, of invaluable help to me when it comes to recalling some of the places in Blanes we frequented in the heady years that followed: Debra, Bacchio, Bar del Puerto, Casino bar, Kiko, El Mexicanito, Ample cinema hall, Can Flores, Centro bar, Pastelería Planells, La Gran Muralla, Terrassans, L'Antic. We'd meet up in our respective homes, but also in these places – backdrops to conversations, quarrels, passions, sparks of creativity, endless discussions, laughter, phrases that slipped away like smoke: 'Smoke with eyes half–closed

E

and recite Provençal bards / the solitary to and fro of borders / this may be defeat but also the sea / and the taverns…' ('The Romantic Dogs').

I suspect, perhaps contrarily, that living in Blanes, going through a bitter time of silence, living in defeat – in adversity, but with the sea and the taverns – must have suited Bolaño perfectly. No, I'm not being ironic. I'm only thinking of the story of that provincial for whom all went well until he got a taste of Paris because, once that happened, the city swallowed him up. I'm not suggesting this was exactly the case with Bolaño but, when I think of him, I can't forget that certain period of happiness some artists have, of glorious, gloryless days lived out in ignorance of the literary world, of the jealousies, egos and the market; days in which these artists were mysterious and antisocial and, however much they deplored living among so much desolation and sadness, lived fully and drew breath in their personal, sacred kingdom of art.

The case of Bolaño's isolation for years in Blanes reminds me of those books Elias Canetti talks about in *THE HUMAN PROVINCE*, books we have at our side many years without reading, books we don't leave behind but take with us from one city to another, from one country to another, carefully packaged up, even though there isn't much space; we'll have a flick through on taking them out of the case, perhaps; yet we studiously avoid reading any phrase in its entirety. Later, years down the line, the moment comes in which suddenly, as if compelled by an order from on high, we can't help but reach for one of these books and read it straight through, cover to cover; this book then serves as a revelation. At that moment we know why we've paid it such close attention. It had to live so long by our side; it had to travel; it had to take up space; it had to be a burden, and now the purpose of its journey is revealed; now it lifts its veil; now it sheds light on the years it lived silently by our side.

Surely Bolaño, just like the book, wouldn't have had so many things to say without having been silent all that time. 'We must suppose that during this period he was building up the formidable energy released from 1994', notes Ignacio Echevarría in 'Bolaño extraterritorial'. To the energy he was building up we'd probably have to add: the happiness of being a nobody, and at the same time being someone who was writing. Occasionally, a period of silence is paradise for writers.

He'd arrived in Blanes with Carolina in the summer of 1985, to work in a little trinket shop set up by his mother at 28, Carrer Colom, where he attended to the customers, generally tourists. In the first months he acted like an undercover detective and set himself to locating all traces of Pijoaparte, the character Juan Marsé places in Blanes with his Ducati motorbike. 'When I had a moment off from the shop and was tired from walking, I'd go into the bars in Blanes to have a beer and talk to people, and so it was that I never found the house from Marsé but I did find friends,' he recalled in 'Pregón de Blanes'.

These friends were fishermen, waiters, young drug addicts (all condemned to an early death) – the well-known school of life. There is no doubt that this stage of anonymity, of isolation, was hard; but it was also I believe providential, for if it's true that, for example, nobody from the literary world afforded him the slightest bit of attention, it also goes that his condition as a total unknown facilitated his full dedication to writing. What's more, I believe the intense harshness of those days, during which he was utterly forsaken, served to strengthen his character and above all his powerful – at times, understandably bitter – style. No one would deny how hard it is to pass through moments of desolation, but it can also be the case that for an artist an isolated, tough existence can prove a severe, if highly stimulating, apprenticeship. This, moreover, can prove useful at the moment he leaves behind the shadows of neglect or indifference and appears in the plain light of day, to the surprise of the many who'd been unaware of him until then... He appears armed to the teeth, ready for anything, hardened by the isolation and the happiness of so many years. A samurai in Blanes. It makes me think of that Madrid aphorist who wrote this truth so succinctly, 'Character is formed on Sunday afternoons.'

I met Bolaño just when he was coming out of a period of endless Sundays, during which he'd been forging his savage spirit; I met him at the end of that prodigious year when a few things had come together to the extent of effecting a reversal for him and his family, that year which began with Seix Barral publishing NAZI LITERATURE IN THE AMERICAS and finished with Anagrama bringing out DISTANT STAR.

Bolaño was delighted. He never lost his sense of humour, and this was especially the case that year. Of that day in Bar Novo I remember most of all having the feeling or presentiment, after only a short time speaking to him, of being with a true writer. And this is something – the reader should know straightaway, without further delay – that is not a common occurrence: 'Poetry (true poetry) is thus: it is sensed, it announces itself in the air, like earthquakes are sensed, they say, by certain animals especially attuned for that purpose.' The sensation of finding myself in front of a Chilean who didn't seem Chilean and, however, so much resembled the romantic notion I'd pursued for twenty years in the real world, the idea of what a real writer should be. Not long ago, Gonzalo Maier cited an essay by Fabián Casas in which the latter, remembering Bolaño, talked of how much he missed 'the writers from the old days, all of those who, like Cortázar, were much more than mere writers, they were masters, life examples, powerful lighthouses to which he and his friends gravitated'.

Cortázar never seemed like a lighthouse to me, but I understand what Casas is talking about. In fact, on that day in the Novo, what I saw or recognised immediately within Bolaño – I don't think I'd be kidding myself to say so – was the hermit-like lunatic or, more precisely, 'a writer from the old days', that type of person I already considered untraceable because they belonged to a world I'd glimpsed in my youth but thought had already vanished for good; that sort of writer who never

E

forgot that literature is, above all, a dangerous profession; someone who is not only brave and doesn't give a damn for the prevailing vulgarities, but who also displays an overwhelming authenticity and who melds life and literature with total ease; an incredible survivor from an extinct race; this surprising kind of writer who proudly belongs to a lineage of crazies, obsessives, maniacs, tormented by the true meaning of words; obstinate types, totally obstinate, who already know that all is false and that, what's more, everything, absolutely everything, is finished (I believe that when one finds oneself in the situation of sizing up the dimensions of falsehood and the finality of things, then, and only then, can obstinacy help you, push you to circle around and around your cell in order not to miss the sole, merest instant – because this instant exists – that can save you); types who are in truth more desperate than well-worn revolution, making them to a certain extent the indirect heirs to the irremediable misanthropes of yesteryear.

These lost causes lived in times when writers were like gods and lived in the mountains like craven hermits or lunatic aristocrats. In those days they wrote with the sole aim of communing with the dead and they'd never heard of the market; they were mysterious and solitary and drew breath in the sacred kingdom of literature. It's clear that the 'writers from the old days' are heirs to the enigmatic, misanthropic, craven hermits of yesteryear; they're like the swarthiest toughs on the baddest street, and of course – I'll say it to add a note of humour, in keeping with the drawn out laughter of all these years – don't have anything to do with, for example, the grey competent writers who, in their time, proliferated to such an extent under the so-called *nueva narrativa española*. 'Writers from the old days' go in search of a highly personal *mode* of expression, without forgetting that within this *mode* may lie – beyond the limits of the old great prose and after the almost complete and definitive death of literature – a road, perhaps the very last road there is to travel. Or not. Or maybe there are none left. Do you think there are none left? In this case, I'll remind you of the line – it's just one line, but *what* a line – from the story 'Phone Calls':

'B also thinks that the street is a dead end.'

Knowing Bolaño – here I add the fact that by 1996, in literary terms, I'd been adrift for years – was like going back and remembering that life and literature, however much the grey competent writers dismissed such a notion with smirks, can go perfectly together just as I'd intuited straightaway in the years I was starting to write; that's to say, it wasn't a crime nor any mistake to mix life and literature, above all it was something that could be joined up with astonishing ease.

I met up with Bolaño on the odd afternoon to walk with him by the sea and sometimes he asked me whether such and such a friend really carried literature in his blood. Even now, his most famous declaration of principles helps me carry on in savage fashion, 'Literature is very similar to the battles of samurais, but a samurai doesn't fight against another samurai: he fights against a monster. What's more, generally he knows he'll be beaten. Being brave enough, already aware you're going to be beaten, to go out and fight: that's literature.'

This tough but also poignant statement could never have been made by a writer without a highly untamed, deeply passionate conception of literature. It was an idea that, as Rodrigo Fresán once said, transmitted, almost instantaneously, a certain romantic theory of poetic activity and of its practise as a realisable utopia... In fact, being with Bolaño on the terrace of a seaside bar was like being with a 'writer from the old days', with a poet, like living this viable utopia.

I look at, I read, I skim through my personal journal. Yesterday it dawned on me how good it was to have written down over those days so many mundane details, so many things that would have been forgotten if I hadn't been noting them since 1985. On looking for what I wrote around 21 November 1996, I found this unadorned but, deep down, highly expressive – for its conclusiveness – entry:

Bolaño.

I also saw upon going through my notes, that, four days after the meeting in the Novo, 25 November, I'd gone to Barcelona's Condes de Barcelona hotel for the press conference to launch DISTANT STAR. This date surprised me because I hadn't remembered the scenes from the 21st so close to the press conference of the 25st. Of that gathering of journalists I recall, among other things, that while Herralde introduced his new author I couldn't lift my gaze from the Faulkner quote that opens Bolaño's novella:

'What star falls unseen?'

We were at the tail-end of 1996, during which Bolaño had finally been sighted, watched, detected. And that quote offered, among others, the possibility of being read in this way. I looked at Bolaño and, in a kind of silent game, I put myself to verifying once and for all that there was nothing in him of the sinister aviator from DISTANT STAR, of that guy who the narrator said seemed like a real hard man, like some Latin Americans over forty years of age can be. And I added, 'A hardness so different to that of Europeans or North Americans. A sad, and incurable, hardness.'

The potential hardness of Bolaño, that day of the press conference, had very little sadness to it and actually offered a perspective that suggested the possibility of a certain happiness. Maybe it was because everything was becoming new for him, maybe because in one fell swoop everything had become funnier and more dangerous than before and the machine of anonymity, with all the energy built up over the course of the days of lunacy, suddenly set itself in motion – the point is that there seems to have been a mild euphoria: 'And so what is a good piece of writing? Well, what it always has been: knowing how to stick one's head into the darkness, to leap into the void; basically, knowing that literature is a dangerous profession.'

E

Around the fortieth minute, by the time everything in the air had relaxed at last, he let himself get carried away by a question about the modest reality of Chile and suddenly embarked on a long monologue – absolutely fascinating, beyond time and place – a monologue on discipline, the British uprightness of the Chilean army. I believe that Bolaño, from minute forty onwards, suspended time. I remember at a certain moment I shut my eyes, and it was odd, I felt then as if his words themselves were heavily regimented and weighed double. Right now I couldn't rule out that the implacable anonymity machine shaping him in Blanes, through the period of silence, may have been doubly-loading each of these words.

It became abundantly clear, I recall, as he went on and on, that he was a writer without the tics of professional storytellers. This became especially evident in the endless final minutes of the press conference when he launched into a sudden and generous never-ending tale, with a genuine outpouring of passion for what he was recounting. The journalists seemed like so many hypnotised fishermen at any table of a Blanes bar and, for a moment there in the Condes de Barcelona, it was as if he'd started a new novel, this time writing it live, straight out, a novel that appeared to be springing directly from the last pages of *DISTANT STAR*. In fact – even though I didn't know it yet – what was happening was the same as what happened with *DISTANT STAR*, which had sprung from the final pages of *NAZI LITERATURE IN THE AMERICAS*...

And so it always was with Bolaño, one book springing from another, everything connected in some way. In fact, *DISTANT STAR* emerged at the precise instant in which Herralde, in his office at Anagrama, asked Bolaño if he had some unpublished novel, something recently written, that he could publish. Such a novel didn't exist, but Bolaño claimed otherwise and wrote it in three weeks – record time, he took time off to do it – and because his work always advanced by means of these unfurlings of one novel into another, a considerable number of words of *NAZI LITERATURE IN THE AMERICAS* too. Between the end of the latter ('Look after yourself, Bolaño, he said, and off he went') and *DISTANT STAR* ('Look after yourself, my friend, he said, and off he went') I think I always preferred that, 'Look after yourself, Bolaño'. But, of course, this is anecdotal. Much less so is that, in the days following his delivery of the manuscript to Anagrama, Bolaño went through some difficult times, and also fortunate ones (he was pleased about this apparent stroke of luck) in which a certain fear was visible in a smile weak with nervousness, as if the possibility the publishing house might discover that part of the text was lifted from his own prior work both scared and amused him.

This whole period, from *DISTANT STAR* on, was governed by bursts of intensity and record time. So much so that sometimes I see him as the protagonist in *SUR LE PASSAGE DE QUELQUES PERSONNES À TRAVERS UNE ASSEZ COURTE UNITÉ DE TEMPS*,

Guy Debord's short film.

'For Paula, with warmth and admiration from her friend in record time. Roberto. Blanes, March '97', he wrote in a copy of THE ELEPHANT PATH, the book published in '93 by Toledo city council. I realise on reading the back cover of the book that in fact it was written only a very short time before the important about–turn in his life as a writer; but not only is the back cover utterly incapable of predicting this, but anyone would find it off–putting. The author biography couldn't be less persuasive, in tenth place counting from the penultimate line of hell, 'Roberto Bolaño was born in Santiago de Chile in 1953. He has worked as a literary critic and translator. He edited the magazine BERTHE TREPAT. His poems feature in various anthologies of contemporary Chilean poetry. He has published three poetry collections: REINVENTING LOVE (Taller Martín Pescador, México DF, 1976), NAKED BOYS UNDER THE RAINBOW OF FIRE (Ed. Extemporáneos, México DF, 1979)...'

From the end of '96, Bolaño's movements seem to have taken on the mark of record time, addicted to breakneck speed. I return to my journal and find noted there my trips to Blanes in 1997 and 1998, trips firstly to see Paula and later, when she'd stopped working for the school but kept her house with its terrace overlooking the sea, trips with Paula to see Carolina and Roberto and to eat, through a long period of strange attachment, in a horrible Chinese restaurant we loved. As the months passed, going to Blanes for the day or weekend became a ritual; we'd end up going to collect Lautaro from school, or preparing to host the close family friend AG Porta with whom we'd lose ourselves amid the most complex metaphysics as night fell in the Bar del Puerto. Jordi Llovet, Pons Puigdevall, Gonzalo Herralde and Luisa Casas, Javier Cercas and family, Joan de Sagarra and María Jesús de Elda, Carles Vilches, Gina and Peter, among others, passed through Blanes in the first months of '97 and my journal, of course, notes the fact. Toing and froing, parties, names, incidents, all was jotted down – even that completely absurd phrase of Vilém Vok's one afternoon in the Casino, when he said that Bolaño had fallen into the arms of the ghost of Humanity...

What did he mean? Oh well, it matters little now. Maybe he was right. After all, Humanity in those days went by train to Blanes.

On 22 July 1997, at Llibrería 22 in Girona, Javier Cercas presented DISTANT STAR and there was a big, I'd say existential – almost like an Antonioni film – party after dinner at the home of Pepa Balsach and Ángel Jové. And as a coda to the gathering there was a highly alarming and unsteady return car trip to Blanes.

On 22 September Roberto and Carolina came down to our flat at 80, Travesía del Mal where they saw the daily pile of letters sent to me for two years, every afternoon without fail, by an unknown woman whose style had become familiar. It always worked the same, she launched the discourse with a reassuring, tranquil, prose; and then she'd lose control of the words and, detonating the bland normality of decorum,

E

entered a narrative chaos that violated her initial good manners (this structure really reminds me of *LIVRO*, that great novel by José Luís Peixoto). Bolaño picked one up at random and read it out loud, suddenly proclaiming – to everyone's astonishment – that it was a very well-written letter. The best thing about this statement were the reasons he found to justify it, almost-convincing reasons that showed how, as a reader, he knew how to find in any text – however bizarre it might be – the merest charm, some aspect worth remarking on.

An hour later we left ours for the alley to the side of the Central bookshop, where a then very young and unknown Alicia Framis (off for the season in Amsterdam and therefore far removed from the fuss we'd make over her work), our one-time neigh-bour in the Travesía del Mal, the only artist I knew on that awful avenue – displayed in the basement of an art gallery no one ever visited a giant work that she'd titled, in homage to one of my books, 'Una casa para siempre'. The board was covered in horizontal black and white stripes, on the black ones an endless amount of words were inscribed.

We stayed a good while in that basement because Roberto said he was amazed at what he was seeing. There was little doubt he saw more than we did. 'It's incredible', I remember him repeating several times, and he made me view that 'casa para siempre' with new eyes and start to come up with all the things that make it great, so that now I'm practically bursting with reasons if I care to count.

On 18 December, in Happy Books, there was a press conference for *TELEPHONE CALLS* and that night Echevarría launched the book at the home of the Institut Català de Cooperació Iberoamericana (ICCI). Vague memories. Not so of the book. Among the stories are 'Joanna Silvestri', dedicated to Paula, and 'Enrique Martín', dedicated to me (maybe because, like the narrator, I'm called Enrique – although I don't think I at all resemble this poet, admirer of Miguel Hernández and León Felipe). 'Sensini', without doubt the best story in the book, wasn't dedicated to anyone even though it was clearly the most dedicatory of all, imagined for the great Antonio di Benedetto who participated like a shade, during his solitary final period, in Spain's regional literary competitions.

The story 'Enrique Martín' isn't one of the best, but the book as a whole has power and presents, among other things, an interesting and complex analysis – in dialogue, I believe, with *THE SAVAGE DETECTIVES* which was still to come – of the tension any contemporary author experiences between the market, recognition and resistance. As Andrea Cobas and Verónica Garibotto point out in their essay 'Un epitafio en el desierto', with this book Bolaño passes comment on the three stale, stark avenues left open to the contemporary writer: shackle yourself with the rules of the market (that multitude of grey, competent writers); remove yourself completely and pursue an underground and unknown oeuvre, like that of Enrique Martín; or, as

E

Sensini does or the actual narrator of that story, or the Belano from 'Enrique Martín', enter the publishing industry but without accepting all its rules, flirt with it and break some of its codes (e.g. the Belano from THE SAVAGE DETECTIVES making fun of all those puffed-up *madrileños* at the book fair).

We've mentioned three ways out, three stark avenues open to the contemporary writer. But in 'Telephone Calls', the title story of the book, a fourth arises, dropped lightly in there, a fourth way and a frightening truth:

'B also thinks that the street is a dead end.'

Did he have a way out before 1996? Two years later already he had no means of escape – that much is fairly certain. At times I think that all Bolaño's principal works, written in record time until his death in 2003, develop to the full in the narrowest alley I've already mentioned: the dark and deadly passageway, without the light of paradise or means of escape for whoever has seen, in shock, and after cranking up the anonymity machine, their wish fulfilled, but necessarily lethal, their star sighted, caught by the vultures of the new land it had crossed into.

Before 1996 there was no alleyway, nor the problem of getting out. Beyond the rough brick walls covered in shades, in the peace afforded his life by the stability of his relationship with Carolina, he could live freely like they did in the days when writers were like gods and wrote with the sole aim of communing with the dead, ignorant of the market; they were mysterious and solitary, lost in realms of doom, humour and poetry.

At the start of February '98 the belated news arrived of the death, in Mexico, of Mario Santiago on 10 January. Juan Villoro wrote 'A Poet', his obituary in LA JORNADA, but the news arrived late in Blanes and when it did, came bluntly, without further information than a death notice, leaving Bolaño depressed like never before; he'd written to his friend the previous summer telling him he was named Ulises Lima in a novel he was working on called THE SAVAGE DETECTIVES.

Mario Santiago left a final poem (which can be read on the wall of the bar La Hija de los Apaches in Mexico City's Colonia Romita), verses which, depending on how we interpret them, seem to reference the end of DISTANT STAR ('Look after yourself, friend, he said, and off he went') and also, chillingly, the poet's own death, the death of Mario, his sudden death after being run over: 'What else is there / other than knowing how to get off the ropes / and socking it to the motherfucker in the centre of the ring / Life beats the crap out of you / it shocks Efe Zeta / Juan Orol movie / Better to get out like this / Without saying semen works or pissing the other one off / Scribbling the position of the foetus / But now, yes / definitively and upside down'.

'Mario was a *poet* poet', said Bolaño in an interview about THE SAVAGE DETECTIVES later that year. Surely, in his position as indisputable bard with the saintly countenance, he was the poet Bolaño referred to when, in the opening lines of

'Enrique Martín', he talked of someone who could endure anything. Mario Santiago was a *poet* poet who learnt in good time he had to know how to get off the ropes. This is the question, that's to say, this is what it's about, *that is the question*: the street is a dead end, a fact that doesn't mean knowing how to get off the ropes loses importance.

'A poet can endure anything, which is like saying a man can endure anything, but that's not true: few are the things a man can bear. Really bear. A poet, on the other hand, can bear anything. We grew up in that belief. The first statement is true, but leads to ruin, to madness, to death'.

'I call those who haven't yet turned literature into a profession *les classiques*,' (Jules Renard, *JOURNAL*). Ruin, madness, death and the great swindle that is all youth are found at the core of *THE SAVAGE DETECTIVES* – this much is known. Less widely known is that its structure takes as model the relatively forgotten Polish writer Jerzy Andrzejewski's *THE GATES OF PARADISE*, as it does Marcel Schwob's *THE CHILDREN'S CRUSADE* (already adopted by Faulkner years before in *LIGHT IN AUGUST*). These two books and *LIGHT IN AUGUST* were practically bibles for Bolaño; I remember the conversation about Andrzejewski at the Terrassans one March afternoon in '98, days before I'd turn 50 and we'd celebrate the occasion at a dinner at Can Massana in Barcelona, where Bolaño would find thwarted his plan to read a few humorous lines penned for the occasion: 'Before daybreak I'd like to request silence to be able to say a few words [...] Today my friend Enrique turns 17, and that's that. Because in literature 17 mean a huge amount...'

Of all the things we talked about at the Terrassans, the most interesting turned on what we might call the 'labyrinth exit factor', these three ways out or stark possibilities seen with such intuition by Andrea Cobas and Verónica Garibotto, the only poss-ibilities open to the contemporary writer; no one who's the least bit honest can keep from asking themselves which option they'd choose and if any of them is satisfactory enough; or if in reality the road itself, as we'd already guessed, is a dead end. There are three ways out: shackle yourself with the rules of the market; remove yourself completely and pursue an underground and unknown oeuvre; enter the publishing industry but without accepting all its rules, flirt with it and break some of its codes, until the wrath and vengeance of the oval office of the literary mafia falls upon the author (read this last line with a piercing look, full of doom, humour and poetry).

In August '98 he gave me, like the 'writer from the old days' he was, important pointers – astonishing, almost – to solve the problem on which I'd run aground in the editing of my new book *THE VERTICAL JOURNEY*. I believed that nothing happens in it, and said so. But he thought the opposite. You reckon nothing happens – he said, puzzled – but a lot of things happen in there, really a lot. (The scene from the base-ment where Alicia Framis had *UNA CASA PARA SIEMPRE* on show came back to me.) It's just great what's happening in there, he told me, full of enthusiasm for my vertical

Portuguese journey: no one has ever encouraged me more. It was an unforgettable moment, because he seemed to have worked out at once exactly what lies in knowing how to escape a situation we're trapped in.

On 2 November he received the Herralde Prize for his surprising novel – for the record time in which it seems to have been written – THE SAVAGE DETECTIVES, which in any case didn't come out of nothing, as some thought, but from the relentless anonymity machine: Bolaño used the widest material, saved up over the years when silence made him strong.

On the morning of 6 December he moved house in Blanes, installing himself, Carolina and Lautaro at 13, Carrer Ample, first floor. In Barcelona on 16 December was the launch of THE SAVAGE DETECTIVES. Jorge Edwards spoke first and next my turn came and I read my text 'Bolaño en la Distancia', which included a series of the-atrical movements by means of which in equal measures I approached then distanced myself from Bolaño while reading; it is an insightful and premonitory text because I predict the compasses which from then on would govern our relationship. Among those present I remember Carolina, Herralde and Lali Gubern, Gina and Peter, Carles Vilches, Menene Gras, Paula de Parma, Ignacio Martínez de Pisón, Javier Cercas. Edwards said that the novel was good, very good, although he had to confess to not having finished it, at which point he received a severe – historic, I'd say – scolding from the author. This scolding still sounds in my ears and, when it does, I imagine that Proust, Joyce, Schwob and Andrzejewski add to it, as if the anger was theirs too.

What to do? For me what resonates most about that period is this question which holds to this day, already mulled over at length with Roberto that afternoon on the terrace at the Terrassans. 'Once inside, up to the neck', Céline said. That's how it is: up to the neck. And one observes how the ways of escape – integration; be an underground writer; enter the publishing industry and subvert its rules – dangerously begin to lose their attractiveness and range. From the outside they seem to be generous openings, but begin to stop seeming so. The alley has no window to the outside, but still one will have to know how to get off the ropes. Any *poet* poet ends up spending a lot of time in the dark alley, will experience a machine of stealthy anonymity wherever they may be. There they rob you, hassle you, follow you, ask you for a light, rip you off, suck you off, scare you, shoot you. There is nothing beyond the alleyway, only the memory of happy days, days in which energy was building up ('I still keep mute', wrote the young Nabokov, 'and in the hush grow strong. The far-off crests of future works, amidst the shadows of my soul are still concealed like mountaintops in pre–auroral mist') with the aim of being able, at last, to have one's say, deferred so many times, to be able to say that you… to say that you were always Jack the Ripper. Yes, that's where it starts. And precisely there it ends.

Not long ago, at the Paraty festival, Brazil, I delivered a radical address on the

E

state of world literature in the present day. I titled it 'Music for Underachievers', and in it I said, among other things, that in fact, with regards to literature, everything is already over; although maybe, with luck, this can be explained, it is undeniable, I said, that prose has turned itself more into a product for the market: something that is interesting, distinguished, earnest, respected but, inevitably, insignificant... The question remains, I said, as to whether writers shouldn't just be read instead of being seen, because I've always thought that at the precise moment writers start to be seen, all is ruined.

The next day the Brazilian press said I had put the Paraty festival itself into question, where so many writers had gone to be seen, including myself. It seemed I hadn't been understood, or perhaps the opposite, had been dangerous and enormously understood and the vengeance of the oval office had already been set in motion. Come nighttime I asked myself why, why all this, what was the point in that radical address proposing the possible ways out available to the contemporary writer who wants to be free. What had I achieved with my tirade? All I'd done is astonish a large group of Brazilian ladies and, to top it all, all continued as before to the extent that I gave the impression – something I wasn't looking for in the slightest – that I am someone who unnecessarily complicates life.

In the hotel, at dinner time, I watched the North American and English writers, so globe-trotting and famous – Franzen, McEwan, Kureishi – and I realised that for them everything was much simpler, they devoted themselves to writing and didn't waste time on useless and seditious positions, old Marxist polemics and all the other revolutionary jargon of yesteryear. And, what's more, they were rich, famous and happy.

When I mentioned this to a Brazilian journalist, he surprised me by saying I was mistaken. Don't think that's the way things are, he said, this morning I talked to McEwan and it turns out all isn't well, he told me that he's unhappy at times because he yearns for the years when nobody knew him and he could write in peace.

I paused for a moment. I smiled. It seemed that in Paraty that day I'd come a little closer, moving with the utmost deftness, to knowing how to get off the ropes. And so it was I couldn't help but think of Bolaño, jealous to think of him free at last from all this rubbish, poet now forever, far from the flies in the old butcher's in Blanes. Neither temples nor gardens. Neither mafias nor alleyways. Free now, like an admirable Trojan poet.

E

VIII

INTERVIEW

WITH

LYNETTE

YIADOM–BOAKYE

WHAT HAS PAINTING GOT to do with love? *THE LOVE WITHIN*, a recent exhibition
of Lynette Yiadom-Boakye's paintings at the Jack Shainman gallery in New York, presents
a peculiar answer to this question. The press release offered a poem as a gloss on the show's
curious title: two paragraphs of prose poetry concluded with a verse of four lines. The first
paragraph announces in authoritative capitals that there will be 'No Talk of the Love Without'
and proceeds to list its attributes: it is 'The Backhand Slap' and 'The Almost Total Abdication
of Responsibility to Another'. Now, the poem promises, there will be 'No Love Gone Awry'.
The second paragraph describes the 'Love Without' as a love of the senses: it is 'a Burning in
the Southern Region' and 'A Sweet Song Sung by The Owl in the Eaves'. In its concluding four
lines the poem turns towards 'What The Owl Knows'. And what does the owl know? 'The Love
Within'.

    The paintings of *THE LOVE WITHIN* do not represent real persons but bodies drawn from
composite images and painted in dialogue with the artist's private imaginary. Entering the
gallery from the impersonality of Manhattan streets, the swathes of rich browns and blacks
on these canvases absorb the cold light of the gallery and radiate warmth. Documents of a
day's work, brushstrokes applied with evidence of regret and revision; other, faster brushstrokes
appear somehow both crude and eloquent. The viewer approaches these faces with a growing
awareness of their lack. Each painting evokes a different gaze but every face appears private,
diffident, almost entirely withdrawn. When a gaze has been granted to the place where the
viewer stands, the bodies are outsized, larger than life, in their scale denying a relation of
identity. The artist has refused in interviews to explain her work or to offer context that might
resolve its challenges, but she has often been drawn out on questions of interpretation, speaking
to readings of her work that feel wrong. If in love a body becomes the bearer of signification
and at the same time remains unknown enough to be indefinitely promising, then perhaps the
artist's refusals are a means to conserve their sufficiency in meeting this demand. Is sufficiency,
for these paintings, a principle of love?

    The interview took place at the artist's home in South London, in a room whose wooden
shutters let a thin rectangle of December sunlight fall across a white plaster wall behind her. At
the invitation of her poem, to turn from the 'Sweet Song of the Owl' to the question of 'What
the Owl Knows', I wanted to learn how these paintings could teach us the philosophy of 'The
Love Within'.

——————

Q. THE WHITE REVIEW —— What was new about
the work in this exhibition?
A. LYNETTE YIADOM-BOAKYE —— I challenged
myself to do things I find difficult. I thought
through the medium very closely, shifting the
scale, to see what happens when something 30
× 30 cm is suddenly 200 × 120 cm. It's so much
about problem-solving with me. I would set
out to think about something quite specific:

how to use a particular colour – like yellow –
effectively, for example.

Q. THE WHITE REVIEW —— You've said before that using yellow is something you find
challenging, but at least a few paintings in
this exhibition had yellow as their base layer,
which seems like creating a difficulty for
yourself.

^{A.} LYNETTE YIADOM–BOAKYE —— The technical decisions become subjects and conversations in themselves. In what I do there are so many things I can't explain, in the same way that it's difficult to describe a piece of music. You can have the lyrics but you can't explain the sound of an instrument.

^{Q.} THE WHITE REVIEW —— I've been trying to understand what it means to approach a work of art you haven't seen before and how to un–derstand the claims it's making on you as you approach it. But we do find some way of un–derstanding all of the decisions that a painter has made. Sometimes it just feels disappointing to put that understanding into words.

^{A.} LYNETTE YIADOM–BOAKYE —— If I think about all of the things I really love, as soon as I start trying to explain why, I don't love them so much. I can't explain why a particular work of art should strike me. That is why it strikes me. The self-explanatory is less interesting. The things that I love are the things that act on the senses, and when you think about how that makes you feel, that is the pleasure.

^{Q.} THE WHITE REVIEW —— Can you embrace the idea that you are never going to come to any adequate expression of what it is?

^{A.} LYNETTE YIADOM–BOAKYE —— It's like trying to express how you feel about a person, trying to explain everything you feel about that per–son. Maybe that's one of the things about grief. Where do you begin? Words aren't enough.

^{Q.} THE WHITE REVIEW —— How does this relate to your titles? In *THE LOVE WITHIN* there are no labels and we experience works differently without the titles. Your titles always seem to be playful, tricky, almost proverbial. They're not helpful in the way that titles can be helpful.

^{A.} LYNETTE YIADOM–BOAKYE —— [Laughs]

I enjoy titling things. I enjoy words, as a separate practice. You've put that quite well. It's never occurred to me that the titles should be a guide to the work, somehow.

^{Q.} THE WHITE REVIEW —— But for almost every other artist I can think of, the title does work like that.

^{A.} LYNETTE YIADOM–BOAKYE —— It's really bad, isn't it? Often the titles are things – inexplicable things – based on something I saw or thought about or heard twenty years ago. It could be as unhelpful as that, but it makes sense to me, it marries well with the image, with the painting. I'm not sure anything would be helpful. You could describe the painting, but then you are looking at it. Some of the titles suggest more than others, but some of them become a code in my head, a way of positioning something among a group of other things.

^{Q.} THE WHITE REVIEW —— It sounds like a kind of free association.

^{A.} LYNETTE YIADOM–BOAKYE —— Writing for me is a separate practice with the same logic. Some people have said I write stories about the paintings. I don't. I think there was some mis–understanding, that somehow the writing and the painting were directly linked. The two have always been separate but parallel. It's a clearer use of narrative, I think. The paintings are not narrative in the same way. My ear–lier work, the stuff I did at college, was much more to do with narrative, because I thought that was where the power lay. As time went on I realised the power was in the medium itself.

^{Q.} THE WHITE REVIEW —— That move seems like a lyrical one. Your paintings conjure a moment rather than doing too much signalling who the person is or when it's happening. It

seems that their power is also in denying narratives. THE LOVE WITHIN is presented with a poem that you wrote. Unlike most of your texts, it's playful but not satirical.

A. LYNETTE YIADOM-BOAKYE —— No.

Q. THE WHITE REVIEW —— It poses this opposition between the 'love without' and the 'love within'. What is this movement? And how easy it is to move from one to the other?

A. LYNETTE YIADOM-BOAKYE —— The previous show I did with Corvi-Mora was called THE LOVE WITHOUT [1 March – 13 April 2013], for which I didn't write a press release. This time, because I was taking the title and I wanted to somehow relate it to a number of things I'd been thinking about, love was maybe a mischievous word to use, because it does relate to romance and those sorts of things, but the mischief was to use it when I was thinking about something more like self-sufficiency or some kind of strength. The title sounds like a mad sort of self-help book.

Q. THE WHITE REVIEW —— Why shouldn't painting be about self-help?

A. LYNETTE YIADOM-BOAKYE —— I had been trying to dig myself into, to bury myself in, the work. Most of the figures are solo; there's only one piece in THE LOVE WITHIN that has two figures in it. Previous shows have featured more groups and narrative scenes. That doesn't happen in this show: there isn't any landscape, there is one painting with two figures in it. But in that work they are close, they're sat close together and they become like this two-bodied monster with three legs. They read as two people but also somehow they don't, both looking in the same direction. So there is something solitary.

Q. THE WHITE REVIEW —— There is another

pairing, in the diptych 'Patriot Acts'.

A. LYNETTE YIADOM-BOAKYE —— It is kind of a pairing. They are on different canvases, so they are separate. I was thinking about being completely alone, looking inward. Drawing on reserves. Maybe it's to do with survival.

Q. THE WHITE REVIEW —— It's very odd to call it love. If there is love inside a person then surely it comes from somewhere else?

A. LYNETTE YIADOM-BOAKYE —— This is a sense of being full of love that needs an object, something to focus on. What happens when the object is not there? What do you do with the love? It's something that you radiate. Maybe it's not the way that everyone thinks about love, but I wanted to get away from romance. That being the only other kind of love that there is.

Q. THE WHITE REVIEW —— It seems to relate back to grief. Which is often about knowing what to do with internal love objects, how to maintain them, how to access them.

A. LYNETTE YIADOM-BOAKYE —— When they're not there. It sounds really mad. This is why I don't like to explain things. This show wasn't therapy, I wasn't performing therapy. It's a rumination, I'm thinking about something. This isn't me saying I'm falling apart, it was more about a certain relationship I was having with my practice at the time.

Q. THE WHITE REVIEW —— It's possible that art can think about some of the same things that therapy, or psychoanalysis, considers: how we relate to our objects. It is the kind of thinking you're doing in your paintings, but still they're not 'talking about' anything.

A. LYNETTE YIADOM-BOAKYE —— It's a particular relationship with what you're doing, being alone, going into battle with someone – with something – trying to bring something to life, and failing, and knowing what it is that's wrong. I've developed a much more acute sense of what that is.

Q. THE WHITE REVIEW —— It seems to me that when artists – perhaps this is more true of writers – struggle to make work it often inflects other, real–life relationships. Every day it is a battle with the materials. If you're focused on self–sufficiency, about this work that comes out of you and out of no one else, then it inflects everything else as well.

A. LYNETTE YIADOM-BOAKYE —— No matter what is happening with what we like to think of as a career, the most important thing is what you are doing: how you move it forward, how you think about it, how you continue to really be excited about and struggle with it. No one else is going to help you. You have to make these things up yourself. That is what I mean by self–sufficiency: answering your own questions.

Q. THE WHITE REVIEW —— So THE LOVE WITHIN is about internal resources?

A. LYNETTE YIADOM-BOAKYE —— It is about posing your own questions and answering them. I think most of us do know what we are doing, where we're going wrong, deep down inside. We all have it. We're naturally quite flagellant in our ways: you know something is wrong and you keep doing it. The old definition of madness, doing the same thing, expecting a different outcome.

Q. THE WHITE REVIEW —— So do you have that experience of repetition with painting? Do you ever think, when painting, 'I've done this before'?

A. LYNETTE YIADOM-BOAKYE —— Yeah. When something is going wrong, it's normally because there's something in it that worked

once. But it takes a minute to recognise that. You can have the same starting point and then it goes off in a direction that is new. That's fine, that works, it becomes a continuation of something, an exploration of something that started before.

Q. THE WHITE REVIEW —— It seems like a good discipline. You're talking about the need to find your work exciting, without looking for easy ways out.

A. LYNETTE YIADOM-BOAKYE —— Exactly, it's doing it without doing anything dumb. Dumb as in becoming so self–conscious or worried about what people are going to say that you start trying to do crazy, unnatural things just for the sake of seeming like you are trying something new.

Q. THE WHITE REVIEW —— That sounds like the path to madness.

A. LYNETTE YIADOM-BOAKYE —— I am often asked, 'Do you just paint?' I always think, 'As opposed to what?' Dancing? Dog–grooming? What else?

Q. THE WHITE REVIEW —— They're asking about other mediums.

A. LYNETTE YIADOM-BOAKYE —— They're asking about other mediums but there's also the expectation that somehow – I get this a lot from art students – painting is not enough.

Q. THE WHITE REVIEW —— But that doesn't make sense if you are, in fact, a painter.

A. LYNETTE YIADOM-BOAKYE —— No! There's a danger of absorbing everything that people say to you and becoming mad or getting paranoid about things so the only way to move something forward is to throw it out of the window. That to me is a danger. Everyone feels stuck sometimes, the only way out of it is to ask yourself the right questions.

Q. THE WHITE REVIEW — In your new paintings there's a lot of attention to the gaze and to faces, to what's happening in faces, the different angles of the gaze. It seemed to me that was one of the experiments that was happening: of the different geometries of the figures within those paintings. I've been wondering whether your paintings inviting us to consider faces are performing a kind of instruction in love.
A. LYNETTE YIADOM-BOAKYE — That's not far off true. I'm really careful about how I posit that, in terms of talking about love. That is the case with the way the show is hung, the interaction between the works. In terms of the sensuality in the work, that hasn't gone away, it has been a constant. In this instance, describing it with the term love.

Q. THE WHITE REVIEW — But this 'love within', as you describe it, is not an obviously sensual kind of love.
A. LYNETTE YIADOM-BOAKYE — It's not, but there is sensuality in handling the paint. The gazes looking out at you, they vary across the works. There are the two men sitting together who are looking out, there's that gaze; and then there's the man seated in the exhibition you saw, with his hands on his knees, leaning forward, there's that gaze. There are quite a few different associations in his gaze. In 'Patriot Acts' a man gazes onto a woman, who looks nowhere. He's looking out but he's also looking in; she's completely looking in. In all of them, gazes shift. I was very aware of shapes in the painting, what shape was cast in each work. That's to do with the angle of the gaze but also to do with elbows and arms and shoulders and wrists. There are all these different angles of gazes and types of gaze and body shapes.

Q. THE WHITE REVIEW — It's not sensual in an obvious way or alluring in a clichéd way. I think of the work as very graceful but there is, as you say, so much awkwardness in their disjointed angles.
A. LYNETTE YIADOM-BOAKYE — They are not portraits of people sat in front of me; I splice the figures together. There's a lot of improvisation, so there is always a kind of awkwardness.

Q. THE WHITE REVIEW — There is something about them that makes the viewer very aware of his or her own body. I had that experience when I saw your work in Venice. I remember a large painting of a woman looking away, wearing a colourful dress ['Switcher', 2013]. I was looking at it with someone else, doing that strange sort of dance when someone wants to look at the label and you exchange places, and there was a moment of consciousness, like looking and considering images of bodies makes us feel or learn to take measure of our own. I wonder if that relates to the fact that you produce your paintings in a single day—is that true?
A. LYNETTE YIADOM-BOAKYE — More or less.

Q. THE WHITE REVIEW — The painting becomes like a score or a map of your movements over a day. Art becomes the measure of our lives.
A. LYNETTE YIADOM-BOAKYE — I'm glad you picked up on that. It's something that I'm always trying to explain that no one seems to get. I'm not saying, 'This is a gimmick, get me, look at what I can do in a day.' It started off being a practical thing about oil paint drying in a certain amount of time and it's very hard to work back into it. People say oil paint takes years to dry so you can keep going but you can't. Bits of the surface start to dry and then you can't move them. You can never get back

to the white of the primed surface. So there is a time constraint there. It forced me to work in this way. I also found that working over several days broke my concentration; the paintings became laboured. The only way to make a success of it was to do it in a single setting, whether that means working from 9 to 5 or 11 at night.

I do slip into a routine. It became a process that I needed. As you were saying, mapping one's movements across a day. As I've grown older I've felt more aware of muscles not working or certain joints not working as well as they used to. It's something to do with how you move through the course of the day, acting out this set of movements and producing something at the end of it and going home again and how within that period you eat and how often you sit down if you sit down at all. All of these things impact on your memory of making that thing. What the painting ends up looking like and how it functions. I think of my working day and how much of that time I'm actually spending thinking about nothing other than what I'm doing. It is really inward. It relates to the notion of self–sufficiency and getting to the end of something, knowing that you can't just stop and come back to it.

Q. THE WHITE REVIEW —— It seems to be a result of this constraint that sometimes there are brushstrokes in your paintings that look very quick – which is not to say hasty – and I always enjoy those moments, so I wonder how this time constraint translates into speed.

A. LYNETTE YIADOM–BOAKYE —— Never, actually. I never feel like I'm going very fast. There are parts of it that seem to take ages and I might resolve one part of something very quickly and spend the rest of the day trying to make a nose look correct. Where people see what looks like a quick mark, I think that

what's usually happened is that I've worked across something through the course of a day, and then there's the question of whether I continue to work this area here that looks less finished and risk completely killing it or do I accept that it is what it is? I often find that if I then, in my own cack–handed way, try and resolve the area without a proper image of what it should be then it just ends up dying, killing the whole painting.

Q. THE WHITE REVIEW —— The reason I say quick rather than hasty is that they often seem to me to be the most eloquent brushstrokes on the canvas, so it makes sense that you might not want to change them.

A. LYNETTE YIADOM–BOAKYE —— I'm conscious of that. If it feels right or it's not jarring, often I hang it somewhere and think 'God, why didn't I fix that?' But then it's too late.

Q. THE WHITE REVIEW —— You've spoken before about a man who haunts your work, or who has been persistent as a subject, and in one interview you remarked that he has become 'more militant' but that you 'don't want to marry him'. I don't want to hold you accountable to your words but I wondered about this fantasy and I wonder whether – as Freud said dreams can be prophetic – one day you'll meet this man.

A. LYNETTE YIADOM–BOAKYE —— I hope not! What I was saying related to a specific painting, a specific figure that I revisited and did various versions of. And I haven't really done one in two years. None of the figures are of anyone specific, I'm not posing them in that way.

Q. THE WHITE REVIEW —— And now it's the love within. Can paintings reciprocate? If we gaze at a painting, does it return our gaze? Or is it the painter that returns our gaze?

^{A.} LYNETTE YIADOM–BOAKYE —— I think in some ways it is me, but in some ways it has been taken out of my hands. The paintings do it themselves.

^{Q.} THE WHITE REVIEW —— You must know you're doing something right when a gesture accommodates different interpretations.

^{A.} LYNETTE YIADOM–BOAKYE —— Yes.

^{Q.} THE WHITE REVIEW —— I wanted to ask you about your absorption in the work. Does it feel weird to emerge from that?

^{A.} LYNETTE YIADOM–BOAKYE —— Frequently! My practice doesn't require that I have assistants. It is an anti–social practice in many ways. I realized early on that I can't really work for anyone. I love people... I like people, love is a bit strong. I don't love everyone. I can't have people around me when I'm working because I am easily distracted. I guard time jealously. I need a lot of time on my own, for work. But then I'll have long periods when I'm with family or friends. Every week I go to see my family and that is my day off. I don't think about work. You do need to interact with life to feed the work. You can't exist in a vacuum. Some people have the cast of BEN HUR in their studio. But I couldn't do it, I'd go insane.

ORLANDO READE, DECEMBER 2014

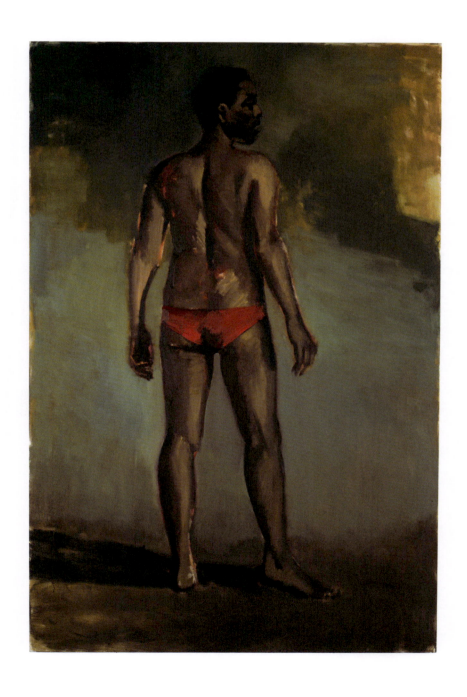

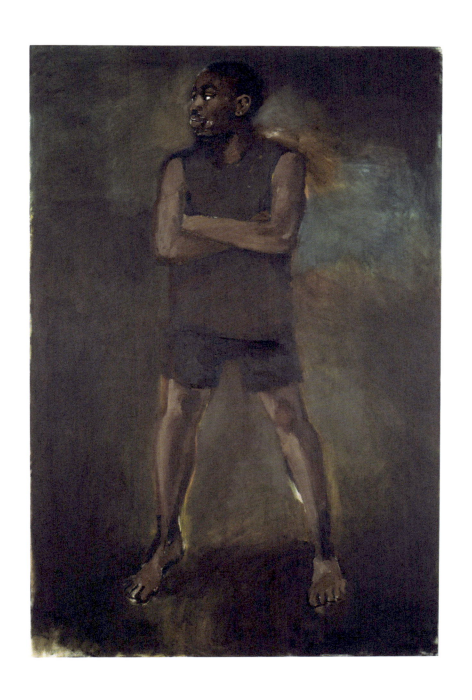

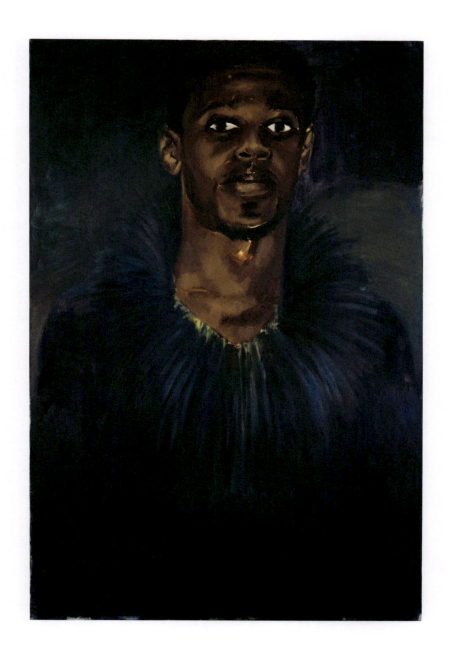

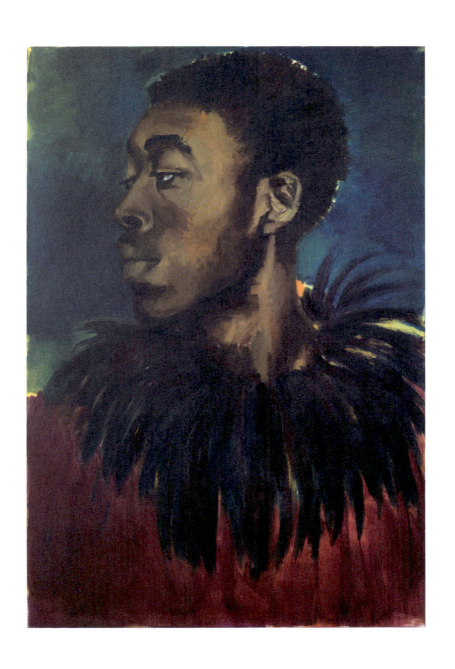

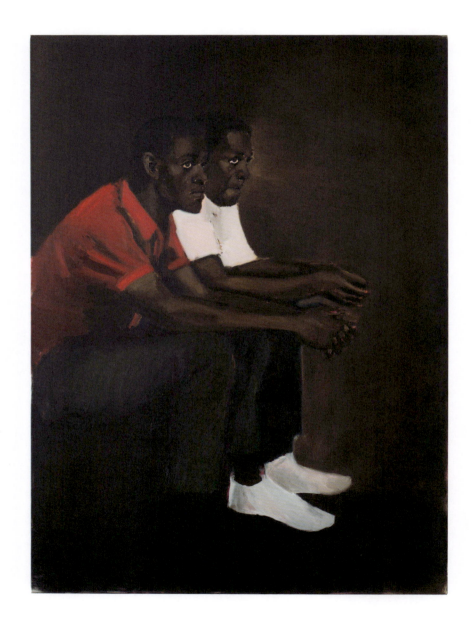

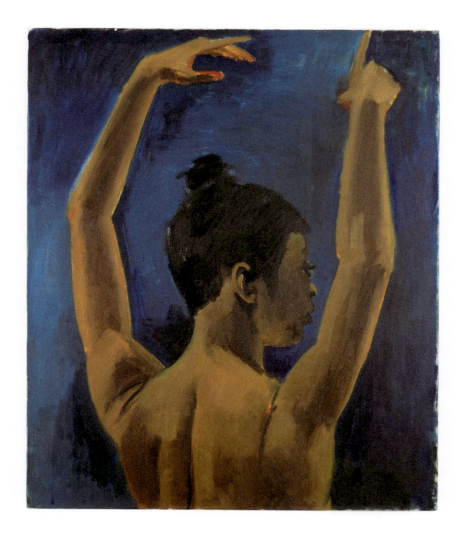

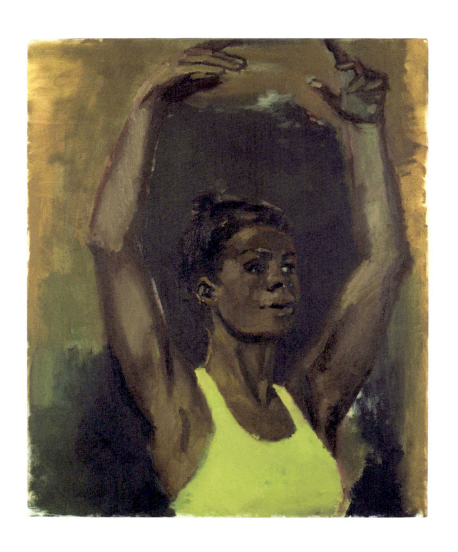

IX

POPE FRANCISCUS UNDER A BRIGHT RED STAR

BY

FEDERICO CAMPAGNA

FIVE IS A NUMBER dense with theological significance. Five are the books of the Torah, five the wounds of Jesus, five the pillars of Islam and the elements of the universe according to Aristotle. The Pythagoreans called the star with five corners, the Pentagram, 'health', and used it as a secret sign by which to identify themselves. On the fifth day God created the creatures of the sky and of the oceanic abysses and 'He saw that it was good.' Multiply five by one hundred, the secular number par excellence, and you get 500. February 1513, February 2013: five centuries that close upon themselves.

In the last days of February 1513 – halfway through the 500 years of the Little Ice Age – an old, feverish man was meeting his end in a Vatican palace. It is recounted that as he lay on his deathbed a fierce wind blew through the streets of Rome. He was Julius II, the 'Pope dressed in armour', the warrior Pontifex who had spent his life fighting to 'push back the barbarians' – that is, the French superpower – and to create an independent Italian kingdom. Having succeeded the weak Pius III, who ruled for only three weeks before being poisoned by his own attendants, Julius II was well aware of the perils of his position.

He would go down in history as one of the most intrepid figures of the Italian Renaissance, a visionary politician and patron of the arts as well as a supremely corrupted Pope, quick to anger and plagued with syphilis. He showed little interest in theology, but he understood his job better than most of his predecessors or successors: he knew that the Vatican seat was an imperial throne, and dared to act accordingly. Having started his career as a Franciscan, the order most devoted to poverty, he had no ideological difficulty in seeing through the religious pretensions of the Church to its essential nature as an instrument of power: the steel blade that cuts through the fabric of history rather than the fiery sword of Uriel that defends the Garden of Eden.

In the last days of February 2013 – at the beginning of the new age of Global Warming – another old man, plagued by scandals and paralysed by guilt, was committing an almost unprecedented act: stepping down from the Papacy. Like Pius III, Benedictus XVI had been dethroned by those closest to him. The Church he was leaving behind resembled him: weak, aloof, sinking into historical irrelevance. Only another Pope dressed in armour could save it. So it was that, as if through a miraculous metempsychosis, the spirit of Julius II seemed to descend again into the Vatican City. The new Pope named himself Franciscus after the poorest of saints, yet, like his other Franciscan soulmate, he understood the operations of power. He even had one advantage over his bellicose precursor: he was a Jesuit, and one of the finest. Part propagandist and part diplomat, part actor and part playwright, Franciscus knew how to turn talks on Love into formidable political weapons, and how to use public displays of humility as tools for high diplomacy. Where Julius II had failed, overcome by the growing pressure of an ever-more-northern Northern Europe, Franciscus was

E

in a position to once again 'push back the barbarians'. His adversaries, however, were no longer the limited army of a French king, but the uncountable, insidious legion of financialised global capitalism.

Franciscus began his pontificate in the midst of a world in crisis. Over a century of hyper-technological nihilism had destroyed humanist culture; the so-called financial crisis had crushed even the comfortable middle classes of the Western world, while turning the transnational upper class into a despotic oligarchy; widespread fear and xenophobia had taken the place of social solidarity. In all this, the radicalisation of religious allegiances across the world seemed to have caught the Catholic Church in a bind, its fading spiritual capital further depleted by endless scandals and its insistent bigotry on issues of civil rights. The millenary foundations of the Church were crumbling. Not only had its physical places of cult become little more than empty museums, but its traditional political allies were in decline. Christian Democrats and Conservatives no longer exercised complete control over the modern Western state, with the very form of the state and the role of political parties under challenge. The Church was in need of fresh partners and a comprehensive rebrand, and it didn't have much time. Great was the confusion under the Heavens, and the situation was excellent – for a political strategist who was shrewd.

Even in this great confusion, one thing was clear: beyond the purely religious dimension, the roots of the crisis in the Church stretched into political grounds, and required a political resolution. When its purpose is the achievement of power, politics has very little to do with one's personal convictions. To consider Franciscus' public, political manoeuvrings is not to investigate the authenticity of his privately-held beliefs. We should concentrate instead on the mark left by his actions and on the trajectory traced by his policy.

Franciscus' political strategy has two parts: on the one hand the establishment of a new network of alliances, with the associated rebranding, and on the other a comprehensive internal restructuring of the institution he leads. Actions belonging to one line of intervention can be used to influence the development of the other, a fact not lost on the Jesuit Pope. Franciscus combines the protean and theatrical qualities of his early brethren Matteo Ricci and Francis Xavier – the sixteenth-century Jesuits who established the first missions in China and Japan – with the ancient Taoist generals' obsessive attention to organising their forces on the battlefield.

The Pope's strategic decisions are based, therefore, on a careful reconnaissance of the global political and economic situation. As he looks to the state of the West, Franciscus cannot fail to notice how it appears to have decisively swapped its modern, progressively revolutionary ambitions for a new/old set of reactionary revolutionism. As the ultra-rich, global corporations and the financial system bend all levels of social institutions to serve their own interests, xenophobia, ultranationalism and repression appeal to an increasingly disenfranchised, disillusioned, impoverished majority. In the words of the Italian theorist Franco 'Bifo' Berardi, himself borrowing the vocabulary of Deleuze and Guattari, the unsettling 'deterritorialisation' – that is, the dislocation of reality – produced by decades of neoliberal, financial capitalism is pushing the masses of the West towards a rigid form of 'reterritorialisation' – or reclaiming of firm land – with ultra-right connotations.

The position once held by the European Left – that solidarity is to be valued above the *homo homini lupus*, and that the concept of freedom doesn't merely have a negative character – has been abandoned. The attitude which Mark Fisher defines as 'capitalist realism' appears to have engulfed most of the mainstream Left. Although the recent successes of Syriza in Greece and Podemos in Spain seem timidly to hint at a possible revival of a radical Left, all the major democratic/labour parties in the West appear to converge towards a neoliberal and bleakly anti-humanist consensus. Only in Latin America does the Left still enjoy a comfortable hegemonic status, while also being able to present the future as a land of opportunities rather than a hostile wasteland. Although it is unlikely that Franciscus has read Berardi's remarks on 'the end of the future' and on the consequences of its demise, he has grasped the immense political potential of reopening – and monopolising – the very concept of the time to come.

Consistently with these considerations, Franciscus has placed his pontificate under the bright red star of what was once considered a revolutionary Leftist worldview. In doing so he has been able at the same time to reinforce his presence in the Latin American countries – partly through a revival of the rhetoric and politics of Liberation Theology – and to present himself as the only credible candidate to occupy the gaping hole vacated on the left of the Western political spectrum. He has founded his attack on spectacularly populist tactics, made even more universally appealing by his repeated (yet slyly ambiguous) claim that many call him a Communist, but that he is no Communist – only a true Christian, faithful to the call of Love.

To secure the previously unthinkable possibility that the Church might emerge as a great power on the Left, Franciscus is sawing together a network of global political alliances within which the Church seeks to enjoy a hegemonic position. Barely a year into his pontificate, Franciscus has held a number of private meetings with Alexis Tsipras, Greek PM and leader of the radical-left party Syriza, in order to devise a common plan of action at the level of the European parliament(s). By joining forces with Tsipras, Franciscus gains access to that galaxy of radical Left parties – including Podemos in Spain and L'Altra Europa in Italy – that look to Tsipras for guidance. Franciscus' Jesuit training shines through a strategy which owes a debt to the missionary activity of Matteo Ricci in China, where the Jesuit priest created a political network by 'converting the prince in order to convert his people'. On the

E

strength of this public alliance with Tsipras, Franciscus was able to set up the World Meeting of Popular Movements, held in the Vatican in October 2014. The meeting hosted a huge array of militant and extra-parliamentary movements – from the Brazilian Sem Terra to the Latin American indigenous movements, from the Italian anarcho-autonomists of the Centri Sociali to representatives of ultra-left trade unions – alongside more traditional social-Christian formations. This event, widely covered by the mainstream media, brings back images of the Alter-Mundialist movement of the late 1990s and early 2000s, and presents the Church as a force capable of restarting a truly internationalist emancipatory movement.

In the meantime, Franciscus has lost no time in organising countless publicity stunts during which he is seen displaying either his humility – by renouncing the luxurious paraphernalia of his role – or his proximity to the poor – as with his visits to prisons and migrant detention centres. His image reinforces his familiarity with those who are campaigning for 'bread and dignity', as when he concluded a mass with striking miners from Sardinia by urging them to 'keep up the fight'. These exercises are in turn reinforced by his public, rhetorical assaults against those whom he perceives as his enemies; as when he attacks the 'barbarism' of European policies against migrants, the 'abomination' of the prison system and especially of life sentences, the 'satanism' of arms traders and manufacturers, the 'inhumanity' of capitalists and financiers who put 'profits before people' and governmental policies that foster inequality which he labelled as 'state-sponsored terrorism'.

This complex web of interventions seeks to re-position the Church at the centre of several interrelated movements: Franciscus is at once a political peer to Alexis Tsipras; a hegemonic partner to the galaxy of radical movements who have no institutional political representation; and the only apparent hope for the poor and dispossessed. This strategy of interlocking alliances goes beyond the plain diplomacy of the warring states of Italian Renaissance – as deployed by Julius II – and resembles more closely that of an imperial power in a period of expansion.

In order to establish himself as an imperial actor, Franciscus needs first of all to secure control over his own empire. His programme of institutional reform within the Church, and his campaign to rebrand its public image, suggests that he is taking the necessary steps. His earliest structural interventions replicated those of Cardinal Mazarin and Louis XIV, purging the Vatican's administrative offices of those members of the Fronde who had destroyed his predecessor and replacing them with a series of loyalists. Such an absolutist turn is intensified – rather than weakened – by Franciscus' reforms to democratise the administrative workings of the Church. Through this process the Pope presents himself as a radical while weakening the Vatican 'aristocracy' and reinforcing his own position: indeed, all are equal below the king.

Such a combination of external populism and internal absolutism brings to mind the recent trajectory of the Latin American Left, specifically Hugo Chavez in Venezuela. Like Chavez, who died only a week before the Papal election, Franciscus promotes at the same time an unmediated and caring relationship between the masses and the monarch – Franciscus always asks the poor to 'pray for me' – and the establishment of a global anti–capitalist counter–power with himself at the helm. Yet, even more than Chavez, Franciscus aims to universalise his message: he addresses the poor and dispossessed as humans, rather than as members of a class, a religion, an identity or a nationality. He has spared no energy in stressing the openness of his new Church to all, including divorced people, homosexuals, transgender people and even atheists, and in presenting his institution as non–sectarian. In his interdenominational meetings with representatives of other religions, Franciscus modifies his language accordingly, to the point of virtually substituting any references to God with an inclusive discourse around Love. Franciscus' brand of populist humanism is literally catholic, as from the Greek *katholikos*, 'universal', inasmuch as its references to Love encompass the universal category of the human, while excluding from its reach only those which he identifies as belonging to the host of Satan.

This remarkable blend of syncretic theology and manichean division between Love and Satan is the pinnacle of Franciscus' political strategy. It synthesises and enhances the populism of his message, the ambition of his hegemonic politics, the modern public image of his reformed institution and, most importantly, the possibility of simplifying the realm of political action down to a division between 'good–humans' versus 'evil–Satanic forces'. Through his alliances and through his rhetorical skill and political imagination, Franciscus is working to create a front which unites all the creatures of God – regardless of their class, gender, ethnicity, legal status, sexuality, or religious belief – against the forces of Satan. The reintroduction of Satan into political discourse has only superficial theological connotations and is not at odds with Franciscus' otherwise modern policies, since its purpose is the creation of a nebulous enemy which is always, necessarily and irredeemably 'evil'. And 'evil', according to the Church Father Saint Augustine, is a category which lacks any ontological status: an easy enemy to defeat, since it doesn't even exist.

We can understand Franciscus' determination to fortify the institution of the Catholic Church. The natural question arising at this point is: why should the secular, radical Left seek Franciscus as its ally? Why should the Left trust the leader of an institution with a long history of connivance with the bleakest reactionary forces and a track record of repressive violence? Once again, I invite the reader to consider this in purely strategic terms. The Left, like the Catholic Church, has been forced to reconsider its strategy by analysis of the current political situation. There is increased support among Western populations for xenophobic, repressive governmental policies against those who can least defend themselves, and the Western Left is no longer capable of reversing this turn to the Right. Mainstream 'left–wing' politicians seem keener to chase their right–wing counterparts than to produce their own new brand of emancipatory politics, and the electorate is growing ever more tired with the homogeneity of mainstream policy. Communist parties are no more, trade unions are in crisis, and bottom–up radical movements such as Occupy seem like awkward re–enactments of twentieth–century scripts. The Left needs new allies if it is to check our descent into abyssal inequality, global civil war, environmental catastrophe and the further expansion of the prison–industrial system.

Franciscus' absolutist Vatican monarchy can be a precious ally to the struggling Western Left. Indeed, that the Catholic Church has kept many of the most reactionary regimes in history in power is proof of the great value of its political support. As an Italian, and as an atheist and left–wing anarch, I can hardly neglect the role played by the Catholic Church in maintaining the corrupt regime of the Democrazia Cristiana for over fifty years – yet, this only makes me wonder what we could do now, with the Church on our side.

The controlling role that Franciscus wants for his institution must trouble political movements that hold freedom and autonomy in the highest esteem. However, without the aid of a powerful, unifying and active force such as Franciscus' Church it is unlikely that in the foreseeable future the Left will be able to avoid losing even more ground, reduced to the role of frightened spectator as the West descends into capitalist nihilism and the politics of tribalism. For too long the Left has privileged abstract speculations over practical, strategic considerations, and the time has come for an approach that achieves the goals of left–wing politics in practice rather than in theory.

Franciscus' discourse around Love and Satan can prove useful to the currently semi–defunct emancipatory project. As the extreme Right rallies the disillusioned masses against migrants, benefits recipients, prisoners and the poor, the Left has succeeded only in creating the bogeyman 'One Per Cent', a force almost implicitly acknowledged as invincible. Alas, cowardice is perhaps the only essential aspect to our human nature, and it is yet to be seen in history that the prospect of assaulting an adversary which is perceived as superior – the One Per Cent – will be preferred by the majority over the option of attacking one than is perceived as inferior – the dispossessed. Conversely, Franciscus' semi–manichean rhetoric of Love versus Satan creates exactly the right rhetorical and psychological effect. Rather than portraying financial capitalist, militarist nationalists and police forces as powerful adversaries, Franciscus presents them as less–than–human obscenities, vermin provoking disgust rather than fear and deserving annihilation. Franciscus' rhetoric of militant, universal and struggling Love radically transforms the enemy into a 'non–being' – in line with Augustine's understanding of evil as non–existence – and thus as the object of a just, guilt–free and winnable assault.

Reconstructed in these terms, xenophobic, repressive, financial and neoliberal forces cease even to be the targets of a concerted attack, transformed instead into unhygienic elements to be cleaned away. How could it be otherwise, if 'we' – the unemployed, the working poor, the prisoners, the illegal aliens, the single mothers – are the forces of Love? Necessarily our enemies must be the agents of Hatred and Destruction. No longer will leftists be forced into the awkward position of answering whether sinking migrant boats and privatising public healthcare is 'good for the economy' or 'bad for the economy': finally, they will be able to simply rail against the 'abomination', the 'bestiality', and ultimately the 'Satanism' of their opponents.

There is no doubt that this conceptual construction of the enemy as a sub–human monster has a long and appalling history. It is the rhetoric of the Crusades, of totalitarian regimes and, indeed, of recent right–wing politics such as those demonising 'terrorists', paedophiles and the 'feral' underclasses. To embrace it is dangerous. Yet we must acknowledge that this brand of populist discourse is extremely effective in the construction of a united front. Allying with Franciscus' new Church, embracing its crusading rhetoric of Love and even accepting the likely hegemonic position of the Church in the network of left–wing forces, will enable just that: a strong, well–organised and financially powerful global network of radical–left forces capable of effectively unleashing the pent–up, reterritorialising violence of the masses and to redirect it against the barbaric, late–capitalist, nationalist 'host of Satan'.

Franciscus' war rhetoric sounds terrifying, and rightly so. If it is embraced by a transnational, united Left–wing front, it might be capable of destroying its enemies, placing the poor and dispossessed as close to a position of power as they have ever been. But it would be a mistake to assume a safe and consistent path that will lead from this revolutionary explosion to the creation of a stable and effective system of emancipatory politics in the following peacetime. It might be the case that, having harnessed the power of the Church to their own ends, the victorious Left will decide to overthrow their old, Catholic allies and to enforce a further, post–theological turn to the new political and administrative framework. That will be the hard path of reform and, as Alex Williams once remarked, 'revolution is easy, reform is hard'. Yet, without a victorious revolution, the chance for reform might never arise.

On that portentous night of 1513, while on his deathbed, Julius II absolved his nephew Francesco Maria from all the thefts and murders he had perpetrated while fighting the 'barbarians'. But Julius II wouldn't have absolved him and his successors of their greatest sin, still to come: their inability to convert his military conquests into a stable political framework that was able to transcend the brutally contingent character of war. Reforms retroactively justify revolutions – it is yet to be seen if this will be the case with Franciscus, the Pope dressed in armour, and his allies.

E

DROWNINGS

BY

HELEN OYEYEMI

THIS HAPPENED and it didn't happen:

A man threw a key into a fire. Yes, there are people who do such things. This one was trying to cure a fever. He probably wouldn't have done it if he'd had his head on straight, but it's not easy to think clearly when rent is due and there isn't enough money to pay it, and one who relies on you falls ill for want of nourishment but you have to leave him to walk around looking for work to do. Then even when you find some there still isn't enough money for both food and shelter, and the worry never stops for a moment. Somehow it would be easier to go home to the one who relies on you if they greeted you with anger, or even disappointment. But returning to someone who has made their own feeble but noticeable attempts to make the place a little nicer while you were gone, someone who only says 'Oh, never mind' and speaks of tomorrow as they turn their trusting gaze upon you... it was really too much, as if tomorrow was up to him, or any of us...

There's that difficulty with delirium, too: you see it raging in another person's eyes and then it flickers out. That's the most dangerous moment; it's impossible to see something that's so swiftly and suddenly swallowed you whole. Arkady's debts were so numerous that when he found himself being beaten up by strangers he no longer bothered to ask who they were or why they were hitting him – he just assumed it was something to do with his repayments. Instead of putting up much of a fight he concentrated on limiting damage to his internal organs. A friend of a friend of his knew a woman who bought people's organs in advance of their death. This woman bought your organs and then made your death relatively nice for you, an accident out of the blue. Once that was taken care of she paid the agreed sum in full, cash in the hands of a person of your choice. Arkady felt his heart and lungs throughout the day– they felt hardy enough, so he had a Plan Z. Why go straight to Z, though? Throwing the key into the fire was the first step of this man's fever-born plan. The second step involved the kidnap of a girl he had seen around. He felt no ill will towards this girl, and this was in itself unusual, since his desperation had begun to direct him to linger on the street wishing misfortune upon everyone he saw. That lady's maid hurrying out of the jeweller's shop – he wished she would lose some item of great value to her mistress, so that he might find it and sell it. Yes, let the lady's maid face every punishment for her carelessness, he wouldn't spare a single thought for her. As he passed the grand café on his city's main boulevard he wished a dapper waiter carrying a breakfast tray would slip and fall so that he could retrieve the trampled bread rolls. And how would it be if this time the waiter had slipped and fallen one time too many and was dismissed? *Even better – then I can replace him.*

The girl he planned to kidnap happened to be a tyrant's daughter. Hardly anybody disliked her; she was tall and vague... exceedingly vague. Her tendency towards the impersonal led to conversations that ended with both parties walking away thinking

'Well, that didn't go very well.' If you mentioned that you weren't having the best day she might tell you about certain trees that drank from clouds when they couldn't find enough moisture in the ground beneath them. She was known as Eirini II, or Eirini the Fair, since she had a flair for the judicious distribution of cake, praise, blame, and other sources of strife. In terms of facial features she didn't really look like anybody else in her family. In fact she resembled a man her mother had secretly loved for years, a man her mother had never so much as spoken to until the day the tyrant decided to have his wife Eirini the First stoned for adultery. He did give her a chance, one chance. He asked her to explain why his eyesight kept telling him that his daughter was in fact the child of another man, but the woman only answered that there was no explanation. The man Eirini the First loved heard about the resemblance between himself and the child and came down to the palace to try to stop the execution. He swore to the tyrant that he and Eirini the First were as good as strangers, but the tyrant waved him away and signalled his executioners to prepare themselves, at which point the man Eirini the Fair resembled ran into the centre of the amphitheatre where Eirini the First stood alone with her arms forming a meagre shield for her face and chest. The man Eirini the Fair resembled stood before her with his back to the executioners and the tyrant and told her to look at him, just to keep looking only at him, and that it would be alright. It seemed he intended to protect her from the stones until he couldn't anymore. This was intolerable to the tyrant; he could not allow these two to exit together. In addition to this there was a sense of having just witnessed the first words they'd ever said to each other. The tyrant feared a man who had no qualms about involving himself in a matter such as this, so instead of going ahead with the execution he had his wife returned to the palace. As for the man Eirini resembled, he asked to see the child just once – he'd never been more curious about anybody in his life, he said – but his request was denied and the tyrant had him drowned, as had been the case with all other enemies of the tyrant's state. All any citizen had to say was 'The last king was better,' and somehow or other Eirini's father got to hear of it and then you were drowned in the grey marshlands deep in the heart of the country, far from even the most remote farmhouse. The air was noxious where the drowned were. The water took their bones and muscle tissue but bubbles of skin rose from the depths, none of them frail, some ready for flight, brazen leather balloons. Houses throughout the country stood empty because the tyrant had eliminated their inhabitants; the swamp of bone and weights and plasma also had house keys mixed into it, since many had been drowned fully clothed along with the contents of their pockets. Eirini the Fair was aware of the keys. She visited the marshlands as often as she dared, crossing narrow stone bridges with a lantern in her hand. She went there to thank the man she resembled for what he had done, but he couldn't be separated from the rest of the drowned; Eirini the Fair swung her lantern around her in a circle

and when her tears met the water they told their own meaning as they flowed from
eye socket to eye socket. Amongst those the tyrant hadn't had drowned yet there was
a great eagerness to be rid of him, and the man who planned to kidnap the tyrant's
daughter knew that if he went through with it he would not be without support. The
tyrant had started off as an ordinary king, no better or worse than any other until it
had occurred to him to test the extent of his power. And once he found out how much
power he really had he took steps – not to increase it, simply to maintain it. A ration
system was in place, not because resources were scarce or because it was necessary
to conserve them, but because the tyrant wished to covertly observe the black market
and see what exchanges people were willing and able to make. Not just goods, but
time... how much time could his subjects bear to spend queuing for butter? What about
medicine? This was the sort of thing that made life for his subjects harder than life
was for citizens of neighbouring countries. Eirini the Fair was sure that her father
was detested. He was a man who only laughed when he was about to give some
command that was going to cause widespread panic. She didn't doubt that if anybody
saw a way to annoy her father by harming her, they might well do it. But she was
well guarded, and it escaped her notice that she was being intensely observed by a
one-time member of her father's court, the kind of person who would melt a key.

The tyrant had orphaned him, had had Arkady's mother and father drowned in
the middle of the night so that the boy woke up in an empty house wondering why
nobody was there to give him breakfast. Young Arkady prepared his own breakfast
that day and continued to do so until there was no more food, and then he went out
onto the street and stayed there, leaving the front door open in case anybody else had
a use for his family home. Two companions crossed his path – the first was Giacomo,
the one who came to depend upon him. Arkady had happened to overhear a grocer
trying to make Giacomo pay three times the going rate for a bar of soap. 'I know this
soap looks just like all the rest, but it'll actually get you thrice as clean....' Giacomo was
cheerfully scraping coins together when Arkady intervened, enquiring whether the
grocer was enjoying his existence as a piece of garbage, whether it was a way of life
the grocer felt he could recommend. Giacomo was not a person who knew what a lie
was or why anybody would tell one; his mind worked at a different speed than usual.
Not slower, exactly, but it did take him a long time to learn some things, especially
practicalities regarding people. Light felt like levitation to Giacomo, and darkness
was like damnation. How had he lived so long without being torn apart by one or
the other? He was so troublesome, taking things that then had to be paid for, paying
for things that shouldn't have cost anything; he taught Arkady patience, looking at
him with wonder and saying: 'Arkady is good.' It was Giacomo who was good. His
ability to give the benefit of the doubt never faltered. The swindlers didn't mean it, the
jeerers didn't mean it, and those who would stamp on a child's hand to make her let

go of a banknote she had been given, those people didn't mean it either. Their other companion was a Vizsla puppy, now a deep gold coloured dog, who began to follow Arkady and Giacomo one day and would not be shooed away no matter how fierce an expression Arkady assumed. Giacomo's alphabet and numerical coordination were unique to him and this meant that it was rare for him to be gainfully employed. So the dog merely represented an additional mouth for Arkady to feed, no matter how much Giacomo pleaded on his behalf. But the Vizsla's persistence and tail-wagging served him well, as did his way of behaving as if he had once been a gentleman and might yet regain that state. The Vizsla waited for Giacomo and Arkady to help themselves to portions of whatever meals they were able to get before he took his own share, though sometimes Giacomo pressed the dog to begin, in which case he took the smallest portion and not a bite more. Giacomo named him Leporello. On occasions of his own choosing Leporello turned backflips and earned coins from passers-by. And yet he couldn't be persuaded to perform on demand; no, he would give looks that asked Arkady to perceive the distinction between artist and mere entertainer.

The three of them settled in a building at the edge of the city. The view from the building's windows was an unexpectedly nice one, covering miles and miles of marshland so that the mass of drowned flesh looked like water, just muddy water, if not wholly pure than becoming so as it teemed toward the ocean. One day while Arkady was out working one of his three jobs Giacomo came home from a long walk, stopped on the wrong floor of their building and accidentally opened the door to a flat that wasn't the one he shared with Arkady and Leporello. The tenant wasn't at home, so Giacomo could have seen or taken anything he wished. But what he sought was a view from a new window, and that was all he took. Ten minutes looking out to sea. And he soon discovered that the same key opened every door in the building; their landlord counted on it not occurring to any of the tenants to try opening doors other than their own: when Giacomo told Arkady of his discovery, Arkady was all for having their locks changed. They could be murdered in their beds! They could be robbed at any time! It was bad enough that they lived under the rule of a tyrant who was slowly but surely squeezing the life out of everybody, but now their neighbours could get at them too...

Giacomo just laughed and pulled him and Leporello into one of the flats that stood empty between tenants on a floor higher than theirs; Leporello came too, and barked at the moonlight as it washed over their faces. Their fellow tenants continued to identify their doorways with care, and were too busy and too tired to go anywhere but home.

Having secured Giacomo's assurance that he'd be very, very careful with these trespasses of his, and Leporello's assurance that he'd help Giacomo keep his word, Arkady's worries were lessened for a time. One of his jobs was assisting the tyrant's physician, who did not choose to be known by her true name – or perhaps was yet to discover it – and went by the nickname Lokum. Like the confection she left traces of herself about anybody she came into contact with – sweetness, fragrance. 'Ah, so you have been with her...'

Lokum kept the tyrant in perfect health, and perfectly lovesick, too. Like the tyrant's wife, she had no lovers. Anybody who seemed likely to gain her favour was immediately drowned. Arkady swept and mopped Lokum's chambers, and he fetched and carried covered baskets for her, and he also acted as her test subject – this was his favourite job because all he was required to do was sit on a stool and eat different coloured pieces of lokum the physician had treated with various concoctions. He was also required to describe in detail what he felt happening in his body a few minutes after the consumption of each cube, and some of the morsels broke his cells wide open and made it all but impossible to find words and say them, but for the most part accurate description was no great task for him, and it paid more than his other two decidedly more mundane jobs. 'Open your mouth,' she'd say, and then she placed a scented cube on his tongue. He'd warned himself not to behave like everybody else who came within ten paces of her, but once as the lokum melted away he found himself murmuring to her: *I remember a dawn when my heart/got tied in a lock of your hair.* Her usual response was flat dismissal – she all but pointed to the door and said, 'Please handle your feelings over there,' but this time she took one end of the scarf she wore and wrapped it around his neck, drawing him closer and closer to her until her face was just a blur. 'Listen, listen,' she said. 'People have been drowned for saying much less.'

Arkady could make no retort to that. She was only telling the truth. He thought that was the end of the matter, but as he was leaving she told him not to come back. She said jealousy lent people uncanny powers of detection, and that it was better not to be so close within the tyrant's reach if he wanted to go on living. He protested – without the wages she paid him he, Giacomo and Leporello could hardly keep afloat – but she shook her head and motioned to him to be quiet, mouthed *For your own good*, scattered a tray full of lokum on the floor, shouted 'That's enough clumsiness from you' loudly enough for the guards just outside the door to hear and sent him on his way, flinging the tray after him to complete the dismissal scene.

He didn't like that, of course, Lokum's taking it upon herself to decide what was for his own good. He could drown if he wanted to. In the weeks that followed that unfillable gap in his funds drowned him anyway – unpaid bills and nobody willing to employ him without speaking to Lokum, who refused to show him any favour. Helping him would cause more problems for them both. Giacomo and Leporello spoke less and stared out of the windows more. Arkady knew that they weren't getting enough to eat but Giacomo to complain and Leporello dared not. Giacomo's fever didn't take hold until Arkady missed three rent payments in a row and the trio were evicted from the building with the views that Giacomo was so fond of. Arkady was able to find them a room, a small one with a small grate for cooking. It was a basement room, and Giacomo seemed crushed by the floors above them. He wouldn't go out. He asked where the door was and searched the walls with his hands. Leporello led him to the door of the room but he said 'That's not it,' and stayed in the corner with his hands reverently wrapped around a relic, the key to their previous flat: 'The key to where we really live, Arkady...' How Arkady hated to hear him talk like that.

Giacomo and Leporello had stolen the key between them, Leporello putting on a full acrobatic display and then standing on his back legs to proffer a genteel paw while Giacomo made a getaway with the key that had slipped the landlord's mind. In his head Giacomo pieced together all those views of the same expanse. Sometimes he tried to describe the whole of what he saw to Arkady, but his fever made a nonsense of it all. Arkady took the key from Giacomo to put an end to his ramblings, and threw the key into the fire to put an end to the longing that raged through his body and vexed his brain. 'This is where we really live, Giacomo, here in a basement with a door you say you cannot find.'

Having thrown the key into the fire, Arkady turned his back on Leporello's growling and Giacomo's sobbing as he tried to snatch the key from the grate. Arkady fell asleep with the intention of kidnapping Eirini the Fair in the morning. The palace watchwords hadn't changed; he had checked. He would be glib and swift and resolute and have the girl at his mercy before she or anyone grasped the situation. Then he would demand that the tyrant take his damn foot off the nation's neck and let everybody breathe. Money too, he'd ask for a lot of that. Enough for medicine and wholesome meat broth and a proper bed and all the sea breeze his friends could wish for.

He dreamt of the key writhing in the fire, and he dreamt of faces coughing out smoke amidst the flames, each face opening up into another like the petals of a many-layered sunflower, and he was woken by police officers. They shone light into his eyes and pummelled him and ordered him to confess now while they were still being nice. Confess to what? The officers laughed at his confusion. Confess to what, he was asking, when the building he'd been evicted from had burned to the ground overnight and he'd been the one who'd set the fire. Almost half the inhabitants had been out working their night jobs, but everybody else had been at home, and there were nine who hadn't escaped in time. So there were nine deaths on his head. Arkady maintained that he'd set no fire, that he hadn't killed anybody, but he knew that he'd been full to the brim with ill will and still was, and he thought of the burning key and he wasn't sure... he believed he would have remembered going out to the edge of the city, and yet he wasn't sure... he asked who had seen him set the fire, but nobody would tell him. Giacomo and Leporello were so quiet that Arkady feared the worst, but when he got a chance to look at them he saw that one of the policeman had somehow got a muzzle and leash on Leporello and was making gestures that indicated all would be well as long as Giacomo stayed where he was. After a few more denials from Arkady his friends were removed from the room: Giacomo asked why and was told that his friend had killed people and wouldn't admit it, so he was going to have to be talked to until he admitted it. At this Giacomo turned to Arkady and asked 'But how could Arkady do this, when he is so good?' Arkady forgot that his words could be taken as a confession, and asked his friend to understand that he hadn't meant to do it. *I didn't mean it. I didn't know* – Giacomo nodded at those words and said 'Yes, I understand.' Satisfied with Arkady's self-incrimination, the officer holding Leporello allowed the dog to stand on his hind legs and pat Arkady's cheek and then his own face; he repeated this a few times as a way of reassuring Arkady that he would be by Giacomo's side until the truth came out. Leporello seemed confident that the truth would come out very soon, and Arkady remembered the Vizsla puppy he'd tried to drive away and was glad he'd failed at that.

Though Arkady broke down and confessed after being shown photographs of the five men and four women who'd died in the fire, his confession was never entirely satisfactory. He got the timing and exact location of the fire he'd set wrong, and his statement had to be supplemented with information from his former landlord, who identified him as the culprit before a jury, pointing at Arkady as he described the clothing the police had found him wearing the morning they arrested him. The inconsistencies in Arkady's account troubled the authorities enough to imprison him in a cell reserved for 'the craziest bastards', the ones who had no inkling of what deeds they might be capable of doing until they suddenly did them. Arkady's meals were brought to him, and his cell had an adjoining bathroom that he kept clean himself. He no longer had to do long strings of mental arithmetic, shaving figures off the allowance for food as he went along – after a few days his mind cleared, he stopped imagining that Giacomo and Leporello were staring mournfully from the neighbouring cell, and he could have been happy if he hadn't been facing imprisonment for deaths he dearly wished he could be sure he hadn't caused. His cell was impregnable, wound round with a complex system of triggers and alarms. Unless the main lock was opened with the key that had been made for it he couldn't come out of that cell alive. The tyrant held the key to Arkady's cell, and liked to visit him in there and taunt him with weather reports. The tyrant hadn't been interested in the crimes of the other crazy bastards who'd once inhabited Arkady's cell so they'd been drowned. But as somebody who had by his own admission dispatched people and then gone straight to sleep afterwards, Arkady was the only other person within reach that the tyrant felt he had a meaningful connection with. Arkady barely acknowledged his questions,

F

but unwittingly gained the affections of the guards by asking a variant of the question 'Shouldn't you be staying here in this cell with me, you piece of shit?' each time the tyrant said his farewells for the day. As per tyrannical command the guards withheld Arkady's meals as punishment for his impudence, but they didn't starve him as long they could have. One night Arkady even heard one of the guards express doubt about his guilt. The guard began to talk about buildings with doors that could all be opened with the same key. He'd heard something about those keys, he said, but the other guard didn't let him finish. 'When are you going to stop telling old wives' tales, that's what I want to know… anyway no landlord would run his place that way.'

¶ Lokum agreed to marry the tyrant on the condition that there would be no more drownings, and he sent Eirini the First and Eirini the Fair across the border and into a neighbouring country so that he could begin his new life free of their awkward presence. After a long absence, the tyrant appeared before Arkady's cell to tell him this news, and to inform him that he'd lost the key to Arkady's cell. The key couldn't be recut, either, since he'd had the only man with the requisite expertise drowned a few years back. Lokum had a point about the drownings being counter-productive, the tyrant realised. 'Sorry about that,' he said. 'Maybe it'll turn up again one of these days. But if you think about it you were going to be here for life anyhow.'

'No problem,' Arkady said. And since it was looking as if this was the last time the tyrant was going to visit him, he added casually: 'Give my regards to Lokum.'

The tyrant looked over at the prison guards, to check whether they had seen and heard what he'd just seen and heard. 'Did he just lick his lips?' he asked, in shock. The guards claimed they couldn't confirm this, as they'd been scanning the surrounding area for possible threats.

'Hmmm… spring the lock so that the cell kills him,' the tyrant ordered as he left. The guards unanimously decided to sleep on this order; it wasn't unheard of for the tyrant to rethink his decisions. The following day the tyrant still hadn't sent word, so the guards decided to sleep on it another night, and another, until they were able to admit to themselves and to each other that they just weren't going to follow orders this time. Their first step towards rebellion, finding out that disobedience didn't immediately bring about the end of the world… The prison guards cautiously went into dialogue with their counterparts at the palace and at border crossings, and a quiet, steady exodus began. The neighbouring countries welcomed the escapees, and with them the opportunity to remove the tyrant's power at the same time as praying a prank on him by helping to empty out his territory. If the tyrant noticed that the streets were quieter than usual, he simply said to himself, 'Huh, I suppose I really did have a lot of these people drowned, didn't I…' It probably wouldn't have helped him one way or the other to notice that as the living people left the marshland stretched out further and further, slowly pulling houses and cinemas, greengrocers, restaurants and concert halls down into the water. If you looked down into the swamps (which he never did) it was possible to see people untangling their limbs and hair, courteously handing each other body parts and keys, resuming residence in their homes, working out what crops they might raise and which forms of energy they could harness.

Meanwhile the tyrant was congratulating himself for having dealt with Arkady. He had disliked the way Lokum had begged for Arkady's life, and cared even less for her expression upon being told her pleas came too late. He didn't think they'd had a love affair (that lanky pyromaniac could only dream of being worthy of Lokum's attention) but Lokum's behaviour was too similar to that of the man Eirini the First loved. What was wrong with these people?

The tyrant set Lokum alight on their wedding day. Thanks to Arkady fire had risen to the top of his list of elimination methods. He forced her to walk to the end of the longest bridge spanning the marshlands, and he drenched her in petrol and set her alight. He'd given no real thought to decreasing his own flammability, so the event was referred to as an attempted murder–suicide. 'Attempted' because when he tried to run away, the burning woman ran after him shouting that she'd just that moment discovered something very interesting; he couldn't kill her, he could never kill her... She took him in her arms and fed him to the fire he'd started. There was still quite a lot of him left when he jumped into the swamp, but the drowned held grudges and heaved him out onto land again, where he lay roasting to death while his bride strolled back towards the city peeling blackened patches of wedding dress off her as she went. She put on some other clothes and took food to the prison where Arkady sat alone contemplating the large heap of questionable publications the guards had left him on their departure. Before Arkady could thank Lokum for the food (and, he hoped, her company) she said 'Wait a minute,' and ran off again, returning an hour later with his two friends. Leporello shook Arkady's hand and Giacomo licked his face; this was a joke they'd vowed they'd make the next time they saw Arkady, and they thought it was rather a good one. Arkady called out this thanks to Lokum, but she had no intention of staying this time either: 'We've got to get you out of there,' she said, and left again.

'It's autumn, isn't it?' Arkady asked Giacomo. He'd seen that Giacomo's shoes and Leporello's feet were soaking wet, too, but he wanted to finish eating before he asked about that.

'Yes! How did you know?'

'I don't know. Could you bring me some leaves? Just a handful...'

Giacomo brought armfuls of multi–coloured leaves, and Leporello rushed through them like a blizzard so that the richest reds and browns flew in through the prison bars.

F

'Giacomo?'

'Yes, Arkady?'

'Is it right for me to escape this place? Those people where we used to live –'

'There was a fire and they couldn't get out. They would have got out if they could, but they couldn't, and that's what killed them. If you can escape then you should.'

'But am I to blame?'

Giacomo didn't say yes or no, but attempted to balance a leaf on the tip of Leporello's nose.

What about Eirini the Fair? For months she'd been living quite happily in a big city where most of the people she met were just as vague as she was, if not more so. She ran a small and cosy drinking establishment and passed her days exchanging little known facts with customers in between attending to the finer details of business management. Her mother had drowned soon after their arrival in the new city: this might have been accident, but Eirini thought not. The river Danube ran through her new city of residence, and her mother had often said that if she could drown in any river in the world she wished for it to be the Danube, a liquid road that would take her body to the Carpathians and onwards until it met the Iskar as it crossed the Balkan mountains, washing her and washing her until she lost all scent of the life she'd lived. Then let the Iskar take her to lie on beds of tiny white flowers in old, old glades, high up on the slopes. Or if she stayed with the Danube, let it draw her along miles and miles of canals to collect pine needles in the Black Forest. As many as her lap could hold...

Thinking of her mother's words, Eirini the Fair had journeyed further up the river and given the ashes into its care. Arrivals from her father's territory frequented her bar and freely cursed her father's name as they told tales that intrigued her. If what these people were saying was true, then the tyrant's drownings had come to an end. It was said that her father's territory was mostly underwater now, that there was no king, no flag and no soldiers, that there were only cities of the drowned, who looked as if they were having a good time down there. Eirini the Fair heard that one of the only pieces of land yet to be submerged was notable for having a large prison on it. The man who told Eirini this paused for a moment before asking if he could buy her a drink, and she left an even longer pause before accepting. He was handsome but the scent of his cologne was one she very strongly associated with loan sharks. Even so, can't loan sharks also be caring boyfriends, or at the very least great in bed?

'Hi, excuse me, sorry for interrupting,' a glamorous newcomer said, as she took a seat at the bar beside the probable loan shark. 'Can we talk in private?'

All Lokum wanted to know was what Eirini the Fair had taken with her when she'd left the palace. Eirini had neither the time nor the inclination to provide a list of articles to her father's plaything. But Lokum rephrased her question to ask if

Eirini had taken anything of her father's while leaving the palace, and then Eirini remembered the key. Just a metal shape on his dressing table, bigger than most keys she'd seen, but still small enough to pocket while she bade her father farewell and hoped she'd managed to inconvenience him one last time.

¶ Just before she and Lokum reached the prison gates, Eirini the Fair looked over the side of the boat they were in and saw that her mother had found her way to the drowned city that now surrounded the building. She wasn't alone; there was a man with her, the one Eirini the Fair had never met but wanted to. They both waved, and Eirini the First held up a finger and then wistfully rocked an invisible baby, motions easily interpretable as an appeal for grandchildren. 'Lovely,' Eirini the Fair murmured, drawing her head back into the boat and pretending she hadn't seen that last bit.

F

DAISUKE YOKOTA

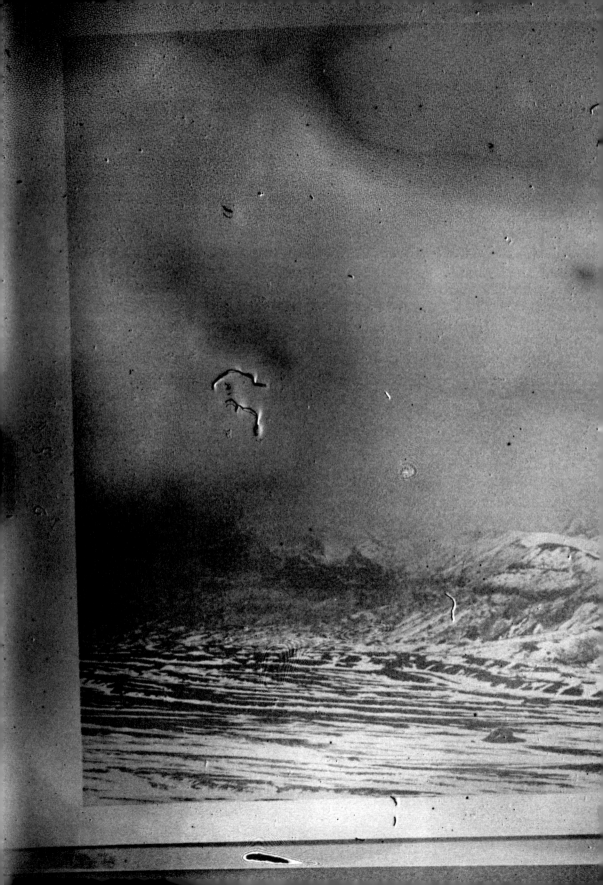

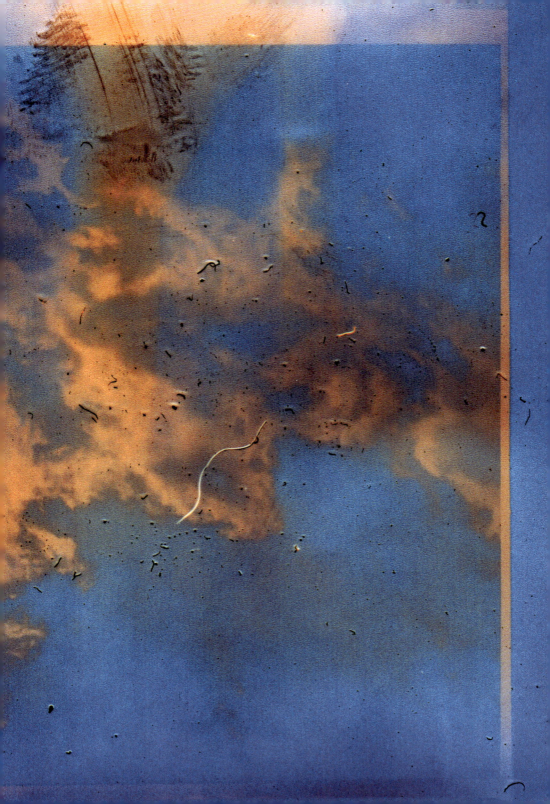

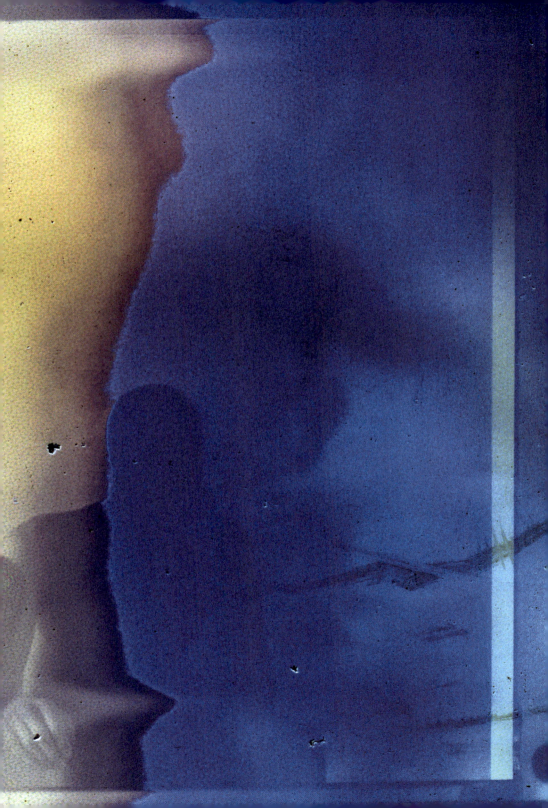

FROM THE ENMESHMENTS & THE SHROUD

BY

JORIE GRAHAM

FROM THE ENMESHMENTS

Still more terrible the situation. I do not want the 3D glasses, friend, it's all already
3D. Look up look out. *Out*–what is that. Will you come out? Can you? Why don't you
try. Still more terrible. A veil of haze. A haze of years. The dancers are
still there. Who are those others? Those are people. People made from a file.
Someone printed them. It's additive. But what if I only want to subtract. It's too
abstract. I have no contract. Cannot enact impact interact. Look: the mirrored eye of
the fly, so matter of fact. Hot tears yes but not in retrospect. Flagstones after rain my
very own dialect. No do not want the 3–D glasses, friend, it is already

                              correct →sun–baked →do not need 3D to resurrect →just
look up look out. *Out*. Can you come out? Why don't you try. You can make you *you*.
It starts with want. Hereby multiplied, commodified →you such a one →created by
successive layers laid down till →(push *print*) →the thing's →created →slick →entire
→it has to be entirely new →once started you cannot be modified →you have been
simplified →singularized →oh look the damselfly →can it land (no) on each of these
wafer–thin strata →horsefly firefly dragonfly →hoverfly →on the gladioli →ranun–
culi →sandfly mayfly → (quiet) →housefly →oh objectified →thinly sliced stratified
fortified horizontal cross section of the eventual →unified →till all traces of the
layers are erased →prettified →creating the sensation of a single solid

                              ground →emulsified →petrified →gradations stations
seams →such as the world. Or time. Sintering, fusing. Such that the thing before you
appears whole. Is whole. Also holy. As in stereolithography. Your friend will be
made for you–your apostrophe–will be all yours–the high–power fusion
of →small particles of →plastic, ceramic, metal, glass →powdery →sturdy →provided
with life →in custody →a series of layers →consecrations →make its
acquaintance →world face to face →will be seen for some time →for your time →your
truism →awesome →must be said with enthusiasm →how do you do, for
example →being absolute about it →historical →the only mortal left perhaps →no
way to be sure →of the custom →earthworn, threadworn →no way to be
sure →among these others →even foolish would be good →speechless →every idea
paralysed →what you wanted →still more →terrible →the art of conversion of

                                        convection of
conversation–how do you do–goodbye–please–(these were the words)–please

thank you I beg your pardon I beg it not at all no I shall be delighted–&c.&c–I am

begging—every time we were more grateful—I could think of nothing else—what
was daily life—what was—my dream—two human beings—confront each
other—speechless—because they can think of nothing to say....

(Spellbound by the history—of god—unknowing—I feel my theory collapsing—I
say *I*—I say too early too late—the Greeks perhaps I say—Suhrawardi believed that
this leader was the true pole (*qutb*) without whose presence the world could not
continue to exist—the world can not continue to exist—he was attempting an act of
imagination—that lies at the heart of—at the core of—truth had to be sought in—
the soul must be educated and informed by—the true sage in his opinion excelled
in—total reality stands before us—look up look out—there is always the world—
a dove drifts by with nothing to do—who is the couple down there in obscurity—
they have sought out the obscurity—it is an immense complex system to link all the
insights—truth must be found—wherever it can be found—consequently—as its
name suggests—for reasons that remain obscure—I shall abjure—mon amour—
are you the viewer?—as such the destroyer—who are you then in layers—
come to take me to my play-date—my interviewer, rescuer, wooer—no—my
caricature—as in here I extend my arm and you, you...

I will say 'you'.

THE SHROUD

I wrote you but what I couldn't say →we are in systemicide →it would be good to be frugal →it is impossible not to hunger for eternity →here on the sand watching the sandstorm approach → remembering the so called archaic →and the blossoming of →feeling the →gambling in our blood like a fold and its sheet of →immaculate →its immaculate sheet →I saw the holy shroud once did you →we leave a lot of stain →we are wrapped and wrapped in gossamer days →at the end what is left is a trail →of bodyfluid →of all this fear →can you feel

it →it beats under my shroud →I have to stop the lullaby →when questioned said yes →said I almost believe you are there →you are there →said the season of periods is over →said hold each of us up to the light after our piece of time is cut off we are the long ribbon of our days nothing more →do you mind →and a crowd comes and looks at the long worm of our bodytrace →in this light →they will see the stainage of our having lived and think it has a shape →it is dirt →it is ooze's high requiem →becoming →soaked with ancestors →and country →one small leopard carried on the mare →and the fluid comes →comes from the cavities →in a few of the lives that stain will be worshiped →just look →the wide light-reflecting light-returning ribbon of one man's days on earth will make the individuals in the crowd who are so blessed as by live virus feel they can be healed. And some of them will be.

The pain you undergo can do that for another. If you gave your life by living it.

In such a way as to leave a trace. To another who goes home to her small kitchen all will

be different from this moment forward. I will change I am changed, I have seen what the

minutes are, they were held up for me in front of the cathedral, have seen with my own eyes

what the days are, have seen what this cup is when I pour the milk into it, have seen in the

passage between cup and lip the secret I now carry in to you, in the other room, in your

highchair, your wheelchair, can bring time into you right from this cup, can bring the passage

of new time in through the new love I have filtered into the pouring. It is not that I

can read between the lines there are no lines. It is not that we will ever meet again or that the

chip in everything we touch is forgotten. It is not that I have forgotten that the sensors

are watching the x rays the mesh the bird of paradise. Now he slides out a twenty. Now the

fireworks go off

by mistake too soon. When asked if she had anything to declare. And they took
it from her anyway. It was her name. It quivered leaving. It turns out she was ok without. So
then one is posthumous. How can I find myself again. In *this* world. I want to in *this* world.
Don't give me the apparition in the air. It is positively marvelous. When are you going to tell
me what is going on. It is going on. The calculations are off. Something was too long. Some
years had to be cut off. It all had to fit. You will never get it even if I explain it for a million
years. One day I'll tell you. Who is this talking now. The rear view talks a lot. Too loud. I
can't explain it now, will later on. Promise. Trust me. Why. Because I made it with my hands.
I made it all with these hands. It is not personal. So you have to hurry up. Or you will not bear
it, will not. How many lights they must see going on now as it is planet earth and we still

have some fuel left for these nights as they come on→
                                                              and we tip over to enter into the circle
light makes→me with this cup of milk→as there is nothing else to give you→the water is not
safe→on the way home I saw mushrooms pushing up through roots→I wish to belong to the
earth as they do→saw an abandoned tugboat on the hillside and some trees still carrying their
colors→wild yellows and reds→as if they were trying to indicate this could still be called
home→in a corner a piece of marble from→grain from→grease someone had shipped here
at great expense→and I thought about that word *expense*→and sympathy like a baby animal
leaning into the sound of words because I had vocal chords→and they asked for that→and
something was down there in me I myself barely owned→but which truly thrilled if a
word was uttered→and I got it right→and how it was ready to declare ownership
over each thing it thought→as if each time the assignment were new→and the visible world
each morning beginning again to dig into my face to→declare me the owner of my
minutes→and what was I going to do with them outside of surviving→having come down to
surviving→as the vague memory of the world you are living in now came to me→down from
what my mind thought→trying to summon the idea of duty→once I heard someone say very
loudly from a podium→the system is broken we need to fix the system→we need to fix the
system the system is broken→and how he spoke of the love of people→and how
unfortunately we could not be omnipresent sitting here today watching you drink the
milk→and remembering the sprouts of tall bright grass growing around the podium→
and how what we saw was their having been pushed aside by its placement there→

I miss the toolbar I miss the menu I miss the place where one could push delete

INTERVIEW

WITH

MICHEL FABER

MICHEL FABER'S range of subjects – from child abuse to drug abuse, from avant-garde music to leaking houses – is as wide as his gamut of characters: be they Scottish kids, Victorian prostitutes or creatures from other planets, they each speak in an unmistakable, fine-tuned voice. His first collection of short stories, SOME RAIN MUST FALL, published in 1998, was followed two years later by UNDER THE SKIN, a novel made into a film in 2013. THE CRIMSON PETAL AND THE WHITE, over 800 pages long, became a bestseller soon after it was published in 2002. In the run-up to the book's publication his publisher, Canongate, suggested he apply for British citizenship so it could be eligible for the Booker Prize. An opponent of the imminent war in Iraq, he refused.

Faber's other books include THE FAHRENHEIT TWINS, a 2005 short story collection, as well as his latest – and, he claims, last – novel, THE BOOK OF STRANGE NEW THINGS. In it, a Christian minister called Peter is sent to the planet Oasis to preach to its natives. The project is run by USIC, a big corporation whose purposes remain unclear till the end. Peter's beloved wife Bea, not allowed to follow him, stays on the troubled Earth; their correspondence interweaves with a third-person narrative describing Peter's mission and his earlier life. Like all Faber's books, this one is dedicated to his wife Eva Youren, who died shortly before it came out, in 2014.

Faber was born in Holland in 1960, brought to Australia as a child and has lived in Scotland since 1993. We met in London, where he was on the occasion of his book tour last October; our conversation took place in a flat not far away from Chepstow Villas, one of the settings of THE CRIMSON PETAL AND THE WHITE. Faber had to call me earlier that day to confirm our meeting as he had no means of checking his emails while on the road. When I arrived he showed me his basic mobile phone and said that he'd only used it a couple of dozen times in his entire life. He didn't have a laptop, and I offered him mine as he still needed to check his emails, but there was no wi-fi connection in the flat, so we proceeded with our interview.

———

Q. THE WHITE REVIEW —— Rereading some of your early short stories the other day, I came across a curious phrase in 'The Tunnel of Love'. Its central character, Karen, is good at 'not so much convincing people they liked something, as convincing them they *didn't* like it'. The next sentence gave me a start: 'That wasn't advertising, it was literary criticism.' It didn't quite chime with my idea of this particular piece of literary criticism, this interview. Was it just a quip on your part, or were you being serious?

A. MICHEL FABER —— No, no, it was a quip: I was having fun in that story. I guess if the themes of that story have any wider significance, it's Karen's cynicism about the content of speech. Because she's deaf, which you don't know at that point in the story, and she's pointing at people having animated conversations with each other, and she's saying, their words don't actually matter. For example, the girls who are gossiping, all they're saying is, 'I'm here, you're here, we're here together. And that's good.' I think for any writer or intellectual, anyone who's passionately interested in language, there's two things you have to hold in your head simultaneously. One is an absolute devotion to language meaning very specific things and being an immensely sophisticated tool with which you can get across very nuanced thoughts – you have to believe that if you're going to bother to be a writer. The other thing is that in many circumstances we're just animals, and the noises that come out of our mouths are completely useless, futile, surplus to requirements.

As for writing itself, I think that even when things are very articulately and carefully expressed, the ability of the hero or the reader to really pay attention to what's intended is much less than we would like to think. People understand and are understood a great deal less than we hope or wish. If you take that too much to heart then you become so dispirited that you cease to communicate. You have to almost trick yourself into not facing up to how huge a gulf there is between one person and another in order to bother to make the effort to communicate. It's relevant in 'The Tunnel of Love', but also very relevant in THE BOOK OF STRANGE NEW THINGS because of the gulfs between the various characters in there.

Q. THE WHITE REVIEW —— There are echoes of your earlier writings in your latest novel, starting with its title. I went back to SOME RAIN MUST FALL and found the phrase 'strange new things' in 'Toy Story'.
A. MICHEL FABER —— Really? Aha. I've forgotten that. Well, I wrote 'Toy Story' so long ago. To the extent of the two pieces sharing any genetic material, I think it's a sadness and a tenderness, a lack of cynicism. Both face up to the limitations of what religion can achieve. The powers of God in 'Toy Story' are very limited, and that's exploited in the story to poignant ends. And in the novel, Peter's faith, the Christianity that he's bringing to the Oasans, is not going to do for them what they hope it will. In both cases I'm not bitter about that, or cynical, or sneering. I'm more interested in the poignancy of it, the tenderness of it.

Q. THE WHITE REVIEW —— Literary critics say that you always write about alienation, in its many forms. The latest novel is no exception. Finding himself on Oasis, surrounded by creatures and things that are hard to relate to, Peter realises that his alienated state grows from within: 'Without knowing it, he'd always been an honorary alien.' Equally, however, one could say that you always write about water, in its many forms: I can't think of a single book of yours where it doesn't play a part. Then again, when I recently picked up FOUR LETTER WORD, a collection of fictional love letters you contributed to, I thought that, in fact, you always write about love.
A. MICHEL FABER —— I don't know if this sounds pretentious, but I think that all my work is about a great many things. A skill of mine is that I can present the reader with a narrative which moves swiftly on the surface and appears to be tackling one thing. If the reader wants to skim across that surface then it will be an enjoyable ride, but if they're inclined to dig deeper then, however deep they wish to dig, there will be more to find. So the books do end up being about a great many things, depending on how much reading or rereading effort you want to put in.

In terms of my work being about alienation, yes, I do think we're full-on-ly alienated from each other. I did in recent years come to feel uneasy about the fact that so many of the relationships – particularly sexual relationships – in my books were deceitful, or exploitative, or dysfunctional, when I myself had this wonderful wife, whom I loved very much and who loved me. I felt I was in danger of compiling a body of work that was more cynical about human potentials than I truly had experienced in my own life. So I felt it was time to write a book in which two people felt true and genuine love for each other.

I've always been worried about sinning against the universe: using my prose skills to convince people of untruths. I think it is a fundamental truth about life on Earth that there are people who truly, deeply love each other. I came to feel that I should write at least one book in which that was honoured. And that's part of what's going on in THE BOOK OF STRANGE NEW THINGS.

Q· THE WHITE REVIEW —This book can also be seen as a sort of follow-up to your 2000 novel UNDER THE SKIN; in both, you have aliens, hitch-hikers, bodies: perfect, ordinary, ruined. What they seem to share to a lesser degree is satire, so prominent in the earlier novel. Reading THE BOOK OF STRANGE NEW THINGS, I kept looking for it, thinking: there, he's aiming at big corporations, climate change deniers, post-colonial hypocrites. Is this all far-fetched?

A· MICHEL FABER —— The book is fundamentally about goodness and the limitations of what goodness can achieve. When you write a book about good people who are well-intentioned, the danger, of course, is that it'll be boring. Obviously, evil is a great deal more thrilling than good. In order to keep people turning the pages I felt that it was necessary to have this tension where you, the reader, are constantly expecting that any time now you will find the sting in the tale: the true satirical intent will be revealed, the true evil agenda of USIC or the Oasans will become apparent. But that's to help you get through the book and enjoy it. It is, ultimately, such a benign book. It is an almost unbearably, heartbreakingly sad book, but it's not cynical at all, I don't believe. It's worshipping sincerity, almost. It's a very un-ironic exercise.

Q· THE WHITE REVIEW —— THE BOOK OF STRANGE NEW THINGS reads like an atheist's take on religion. The main characters are your archetypal Christian do-gooders, and not very likeable at that. Bea is obsessed with squabbles in their church and prays for a steady supply of chocolate; Peter strives to be holier-than-thou: 'He didn't want to be like some old-fashioned imperialist missionary, poncing about like Moses in a safari suit, capitalising on a mis-conception that he was from the same tribe as Jesus and that God was an Englishman.' Are you satirising religion here?

A· MICHEL FABER —— I'm an atheist, but I'm not trying to satirise it at all. And what I want to ask you is: if you went to a pub in a city that you didn't know particularly well, and you were given a spiked drink, and you lost all consciousness, and you were robbed and raped and beaten up and left in the street, and every-one assumed you were drunk, who would be most likely to come and help you?

Q· THE WHITE REVIEW —— I haven't got enough data to give you a statistically significant answer.

A· MICHEL FABER —— I think it's statistically more likely to be a Christian.

Q· THE WHITE REVIEW —— Where we live that's probably the case. You have to respect those Christians who spend their lives helping others. Unfortunately, their help often comes with a certain degree of brainwashing – as exemplified by Bea's and Peter's good deeds. Take the episode when they start talking to a family in turmoil, sincerely wanting to calm things down: 'They'd done this hundreds of times before. Conversation, genuine unforced conversation, but with the potential to become something much more significant if the mom-ent arose when it was right to mention Jesus.' If a conversation really is genuine and unforced, why stress that?

A. MICHEL FABER —— You're being too harsh on human beings there. If someone picks you up from the gutter they're not pretending to be a Good Samaritan – they *are* being a Good Samaritan.

Q. THE WHITE REVIEW —— Have you ever been in a similar situation?

A. MICHEL FABER —— I've been helped by people who've got sincere Christian faith. And I can't have that faith myself – it's just not possible for me, intellectually or emotionally. But at this point in my life it would just be wrong for me to sneer, it really would. I mean sneering as a form of satire, because when you satirise something you fundamentally distrust what you're pretending to be praising. I didn't want to do that sort of satire in this book. I wanted my admiration for both Peter and Bea to be honest.

Q. THE WHITE REVIEW —— The Bible is central to the book. As Peter, a reformed alcoholic, preaches to his flock, they all get drunk on 'King James liquor – the real stuff'. I take it you didn't grow up with it?

A. MICHEL FABER —— I was a Christian when I was younger. I lost my faith at the age of 12 or something, and left a letter on the kitchen table telling my parents that I'd lost my faith.

Writers keep reading the King James Bible because there's some marvellous prose in it. I've remained interested not just in its poetic language, but also in issues of faith. I have returned to the Bible a number of times, out of curiosity or ongoing fascination, even though it doesn't have a religious significance for me. But it has a literary one and a philosophical one. It's a book that grapples with big issues and, in that sense, is key in our culture.

Q. THE WHITE REVIEW —— What was your parents' response to that letter?

A. MICHEL FABER —— My mother was very aggrieved that she wouldn't meet me in heaven. My father said that I would have to go to the church and tell them myself – to officially wind up my involvement with the church library, because I ran the church library at the age of 12.

My faith was eroded very slowly. It was the usual intellectual thing where you read the Bible with a critical eye and you realise that this just cannot be literally true – it has to be a metaphor, a fable of some sort. And of course, once you come to that position, you're no longer a mainstream Christian. You could, I guess, be some sort of Christian, but most forms of Christianity do require you to believe that it is literally true. And I just couldn't anymore.

Q. THE WHITE REVIEW —— One of the characters in *THE BOOK OF STRANGE NEW THINGS* says of his religious beliefs: 'I'm nothing. And that's the way it's staying.' Has writing this book changed your atheism in any way?

A. MICHEL FABER —— Let me answer that another way. I don't believe that Eva lives on: I think she's dead, and I think that her body is ash, and that is all it is. Nothing that I've written in this book or experienced during the process of losing her has made me any more prone to believing that there's a spirit that lives on, or there's something mysterious that science cannot explain. In that sense, I'm still trapped in the same materialist universe I was trapped in when I began to write the book, which I'm very sad about; I don't wish to live in a materialist universe. But that's what I believe.

Q. THE WHITE REVIEW —— And it is as a

materialist that you cross sci-fi with literary fiction? Your books are full of various elements of the genre.

A. MICHEL FABER — Certainly several of them; I mean, clearly there's no sci-fi in *THE CRIMSON PETAL AND THE WHITE*.

Q. THE WHITE REVIEW — Except that its narrator is a time traveller, our contemporary transported into the nineteenth century – and not just because of his candid descriptions of bodily functions: he knows more than was possible for anyone to know in 1875.

A. MICHEL FABER — You – the reader – have been transported into the nineteenth century. Does that make it a sci-fi book? Well, in a way. There's a book by Charles Palliser called *THE QUINCUNX*. It purports to be a book written in the nineteenth century which was lost and rediscovered. I never wanted that kind of pretence with *THE CRIMSON PETAL*. I clearly wanted a book written with all the knowledge that we have, post-twentieth century, post-Freudianism, post-feminism.

Q. THE WHITE REVIEW — Otherwise you could have used a more stylised language.

A. MICHEL FABER — Yes, it could have been more stylised. But I was actually basing the dialogue on private correspondence between nineteenth-century people who spoke more plainly, unaffectedly and frankly in private correspondence than they did in the sort of prose that gets handed down to us from more public sources. So I think the dialogue was genuinely nineteenth-century, in that real people then could talk like that. But yes, the prose surrounding the dialogue – a lot of that was more modern than you would find in a nineteenth-century book. That was part of me not wishing to make a faux-Victorian novel. It was more a modern novel that happened to be

set in 1875. And yes, in that sense it becomes a time-travelling book. And of course, at the very beginning of it there is that phrase, 'you are an alien from another time and place altogether', which could equally apply to any of my books.

Q. THE WHITE REVIEW — Why do you tend to choose sci-fi as a device? Does it help you convey certain things?

A. MICHEL FABER — I read very little fiction of any kind these days, and I certainly haven't read any genre fiction for twenty-five years. It's not because I have contempt for it; it's just that I'm not reading much, and if I do read I want to read something that's going to take me somewhere I've never been before. Whereas the whole point of genre fiction is that it takes you where you've been before – that's what people rely on. By the same token, I don't want to write boring literary fiction. Because there are an awful lot of very, very boring literary novels out there, and quite a number of them end up on the Booker shortlist.

I think that *my* ideal reader wants to have fun, you know, they want to have thrills. And if I can give them thrills via certain sci-fi elements, elements of gothic melodrama or mystery, then I think it's a perfectly clean transaction. I will choose those elements which excite *me*, so it's not that I'm thinking, in a calculating and condescending way, oh, this is the sort of stuff that people less clever than me might enjoy. I'm putting in there the things that I would find intriguing or thrilling if I read such a book. I want the books to have all the spills and thrills, but I also want them to have the depth. And I don't see why they can't have everything, why they can't also be vividly described, why the characters shouldn't have depth and why the dialogue shouldn't be well-sprung. My ambition is for the books to work on all the levels that a book can work on.

Q. THE WHITE REVIEW —— The best example of that is UNDER THE SKIN: a sci–fi thriller as well as a satire on contemporary society, a comment on killing animals, first of all, but also on a number of other things, including feminism. While you clearly sympathise with the cause, would it be fair to say that there is a certain ironic note in your take on feminism?

A. MICHEL FABER —— None of my books except the unpublished BOMBSHELL and THE SHIP OF FOOLS has a self-conscious political or ideological agenda, and who knows, maybe the fact that those two books had such an agenda was the reason I didn't push for them to be published. Instead, I've been concerned to illuminate various emotional, spiritual and psychological states in unique individuals. Feminism is relevant to UNDER THE SKIN in that its heroine, Isserley, has huge disempowered resentments against the males of her own species while killing the males of another. But the book is more concerned with alienation: she has no hope of relating to these victims because she has categorised them as non–human and generic, whereas the reader can see that they are men of very different kinds and potentials. For purely arbitrary reasons, Isserley spares some men who are nasty shits while choosing to kill others who are sympathetic sweeties. You might argue that this is a parody of the Andrea Dworkin approach – 'all men are equally abhorrent to me' – but that wasn't my intention.

Q. THE WHITE REVIEW —— What did you think of Jonathan Glazer's interpretation of your novel?

A. MICHEL FABER —— Glazer's film is bleaker than the novel, but I liked it very much. I was delighted that he diverged from my novel so radically; I would have been sorely disappointed if he'd tried to be faithful to it because the book does what it does better than any movie could and the result would therefore have been a mediocre work of art, and we don't need yet more mediocre art in the world. One thing that the film brings out very strongly that's only touched upon in the book is what violent rape is all about. The unnamed Isserley–character's assailant literally pulls her skin off. This is so clearly an assault that has nothing to do with sexual attraction and everything to do with power.

Q. THE WHITE REVIEW —— Power is an important motif in THE CRIMSON PETAL AND THE WHITE, where it is still overwhelmingly the privilege of men. However, 'the march of progress' is already underway. The characters 'are on a fast train to the twentieth century': a woman called Emmeline prepared to 'take her life into her hands, by offering it' to a man she desires; a little girl who wants to be a 'lady explorer'; a prostitute working on an autobiographical novel whose working titles include WOMEN AGAINST MEN. In a scene where the protagonist, aged 7, reads 'grown–up poetry' for the first time (her mother, tired of her favourite nursery rhyme, gives her a volume of Rochester) she feels 'only an odour of male superiority clinging to her brain'. Yet over a decade later, rereading her own angry writing – 'Vile man, eternal Adam, I indict you!' – she bites her lip in embarrassment. Is Sugar's feminist stance less dogmatic, more mature than that of many of her successors?

A. MICHEL FABER —— THE CRIMSON PETAL is my most feminist book, in that I started writing it when I was 19 and newly married to a woman who'd been a lesbian before she met me, and my whole circle of acquaintance seemed to be radicalised gays who accepted me as a sort of honorary female. And it was the late 1970s and feminism was very much in the air. Sugar's growth throughout the book reflects my own as years passed. When researching THE CRIMSON PETAL, I tried to stick to primary sources as much as I could, rather than reading too many twentieth-century interpretations and analyses of the Victorians. Some of the examples of nineteenth-century males' condescension and disrespect against women made me furious, but on the other hand, nineteenth-century middle-class women had some advantages that their modern counterparts don't. Again, my concern was not so much to dissect a bygone socio-political system but to invite the modern reader to ask questions about how they wish to live their own life, how they relate to the opposite sex, what values sustain them, and so on. There is a broader enquiry in that book about the tension between reforming society as a whole and making progress within oneself as a human being.

Radical certainties can't survive the complex sadnesses of real life. We are all damaged human beings struggling to get by. There are lovely, gracious, empathetic men in the world and brutish, mean-spirited, poisonous women. The character of Peter in THE BOOK OF STRANGE NEW THINGS is partly intended to correct any conception that readers might have of me as an author who writes about strong admirable women and weak disappointing men.

Q. THE WHITE REVIEW —— That takes us back to your intention to make your books multi-layered: THE BOOK OF STRANGE NEW THINGS does provoke the reader to think about eternal subjects, but it also works as a page-turner – up to a point where the ending becomes almost inevitable. Even the chapter titles, each match-ing the last phrase of the chapter, become more and more revealing. One thing the reader still doesn't know, though, is what happens to Peter: does he go back or does he go native?

A. MICHEL FABER —— One way of interpret-ing it is that he fell in love with a woman, and whatever the woman was, he followed. Because there's a possible reading of Peter that sees him as an immensely weak man who just gets carried along by the tide around him. There's another reading of him, which is that he's a tremendously principled man and can resist temptations of lots of different kinds. Yet another reading is that he's actually a psycho-path, a highly manipulative type. And as a minister who's trying to win souls he has to have an element of manipulativeness. If some-one wished to read Peter in this way he could be seen as an arch-manipulator who just likes to come across as a nice guy.

Q. THE WHITE REVIEW —— One role that he takes upon himself is that of a translator. He rewrites the Bible for the Oasans, to eliminate the sibilants that they can't pronounce, as well as to bridge certain cultural gaps between their experience and that of the evangelists – or rather, of the English translators. I liked your Oulipo-style experiment with Pidgin English.

A. MICHEL FABER —— A book as sad as this needs humour to provide relief and consola-tion. I think the whole translation of the King James Bible into Oasan-friendly, simplified English is lots of fun. When I was a child, and a Christian, I read a lot of Christian lit-erature written in Pidgin English. There's a lot of that in New Guinea, which is a neighbour of Australia, so a lot of the evangelist effort from Australian Christians was focused on New Guinea. I've got THREE LITTLE PIGS in Pidgin at home – I've got a record of it, it's ter-rific. *Tripela Liklik Pik* or something – I don't remember it off by heart.

Q. THE WHITE REVIEW — Is that why you are interested in linguistic quirks? Or because of your bilingual background? One of your short stories is called 'Pidgin American'. In *THE COURAGE CONSORT*, you have a Belgian character with an incredibly heavy accent, which is used for comic effect, but the main purpose of this device seems to be broader.

A. MICHEL FABER — My father learned English from Linguaphone records. You'd buy a seven-inch record and you'd copy the pronunciation of the person teaching you the foreign language. So my father would put on this little record and a man with a very exaggerated BBC English accent would say: 'This is my family: my wife, my daughter, and I.' And my father in his Dutchness would sit there solemnly, copying this accent, thinking that it would help him in some way – in Australia, where, of course, nobody talked like that and people would laugh if you did.

Q. THE WHITE REVIEW — Did he keep his Dutch accent?

A. MICHEL FABER — Yes, oh yes. Towards the end of his life, just a few years before he died, he mastered the 'th' sound. It's quite an achievement, if you haven't mastered it young, to master it later on. But yes, he always spoke with a thick accent. And my mother's English was very poor, always.

Q. THE WHITE REVIEW — You were 7 when you moved to Australia. I presume that was when you first started to learn English? How did it react with your Dutch? Would you say that your prose is, to an extent, a product of the two?

A. MICHEL FABER — As far as I'm aware, my parents didn't forewarn me, when we emigrated, that Australians would be speaking a different language. So English was a shock. I

learned it fast, of course, as children do. And possibly learned it better than I strictly needed to.

I'm not sure how to characterise my English. The first 'book' I wrote, at the age of 8, was called *KNABBEL EN BABBEL GO TO THE MOON*, and it mixed English and Dutch quite innocently. I doubt there's any Dutch left in my prose now. It's probably more Australian than British.

Q. THE WHITE REVIEW — So why is it important for you to have some linguistic play in your prose?

A. MICHEL FABER — Again, I want the reader to have amusement, so it's another way of entertaining. It's also another aspect of difficulty in communicating, and the poignancy of people imagining that they are understood better than they really are understood, or that they are respected more than they really are respected. I guess if there's a motto hanging over my work altogether, it would be 'Know Thyself'. So many of my characters lack the knowledge that they would need in order to get by.

Q. THE WHITE REVIEW — The protagonist of 'Pidgin American', a Polish girl, uses her accent to her advantage, turning it up or down when necessary. She also sees through a potential one–night stand: 'All he wanted from her was sex. His clubfooted inability to vault over the language barrier and his typically British fear of deep waters rendered him harmless compared to her friends in Poland, who all wanted much, much more from her than mere sex.' You are not the first to criticise the Brits for their linguistic backwardness.

A. MICHEL FABER — That I have two languages is no credit to me: I was born into one and went to the other. It's not as if I've made an effort to learn another language as an adult, so I can't be censorious of the Brits for not making the effort to learn other European languages. But I do think it's extraordinary that, for example, the British and the Americans would be happy to commit trillions of dollars, pounds to an overseas war where they destroy the infrastructure of a foreign country, maim and kill many of its people, without speaking that language or having any idea of who these are, not knowing how they relate to each other, what the factions are in this country. It's extraordinary that it's seen as unnecessary to understand what these people are saying and thinking before embarking on this enormously expensive and destructive project. And that really says something about linguistic arrogance.

Q. THE WHITE REVIEW —— One of the characters in THE BOOK OF STRANGE NEW THINGS, Peter's predecessor, the first man ever to preach to the Oasans, is called Kurtzberg. In the acknowledgements you say it's a nod to 'that pioneer of new universes', the American comic artist Jack Kirby. Could this character also be read as a reference to Mistah Kurtz?

A. MICHEL FABER —— Of course Kurtz is in there too – in both his HEART OF DARKNESS and APOCALYPSE NOW incarnations. All my books are multi-layered, but I try not to load them up with the metatextual signposts that call attention to their multi-layeredness.

Q. THE WHITE REVIEW —— Peter eventually starts preaching to the Oasans in their own language. I tried to decode your Oasan passages, but failed. Could you read some of them for me?

A. MICHEL FABER —— No, I don't have a glossary, I have no idea what he's saying to them or what they're saying to him. And I

can't read it – I have a larynx and a tongue and vocal cords; the Oasans don't. I've been working with the avant-garde musician Andrew Liles, who is these days basically half of the group called Nurse With Wound. He offered to organise some technology for me, whereby I could do readings from THE BOOK OF STRANGE NEW THINGS and whenever I had to do an Oasan voice I would press a foot pedal, and my voice would be distorted in a particular way. But the distortion pedal just didn't sound right. The problem has now been solved, sort of, by default. I'd hoped that technology could come to my rescue but in the end, I was asked by radio interviewers to read out particular sections of the book and I was obliged to do it with my voice alone. I pronounce these 'unpronounceable' letters in a strangled manner, trying to keep my tongue immobile. It sounds nothing like an Oasan, but it sounds tortured, which I suppose is better than nothing.

Q. THE WHITE REVIEW —— One of the questions you're supposed to ask a writer in an interview like this is about the way they physically write. I feel it's especially apt in your case – I don't even know how you produced that Oasan script.

A. MICHEL FABER —— In my original typescript on the computer the Oasan characters are from the Thai alphabet. In the final copy you've got here they are specifically designed by Canongate. I'm 54 now, I started writing in the days before computers and didn't have a typewriter, so my manuscripts show a very characteristic twentieth-century progression: I handwrote THE CRIMSON PETAL on foolscap paper, which isn't manufactured anymore, I wrote it with a ball-point pen in a very tiny handwriting, and because I was unaware that Tipp-Ex had been invented I would use white

house paint to make the deletions, which
would mean I would have to wait 45 minutes
for the house paint to dry, and I would touch it
with my finger to see if it was dry yet, and so
on. Then as soon as computers were invented
I used computers. I now compose entirely on
computers, so there's no such thing as a draft
anymore because I'm constantly revising as I
write.

We should probably talk in the past tense
now. The way I used to work is that I would
write a chapter and I would print it out for
Eva, my wife, and she would read it and
she would give me feedback, and we would
discuss it in great detail for hours or days. And
then I would go back and see which of her
suggestions I could draft into the next version,
and then I would print it out again and show
it to her, and so on. But now that she is dead,
that's not going to happen anymore. Also, I
believe that this is my last novel. So...

Q. THE WHITE REVIEW —— Does that mean you
are going to return to short stories?
A. MICHEL FABER —— I would continue to write
short stories if a short story suggested itself. If
in time I find that I've written enough good–
quality short stories for another collection,
there could be be another collection. I'm also
writing poetry now, specifically as part of
the grieving process of losing my wife. In the
future I might also write non–fiction. There
are various projects I have in mind, which
would not be commercial projects, they'd be
of interest to very few people. Also, Eva left
behind a great deal of unfinished writing. At
some point I'll see what happens if I try to
finish that – if I collaborate with her after her
death.

ANNA ASLANYAN, FEBRUARY 2015

THE MARK
AND THE VOID

BY

PAUL MURRAY

'Claude?'

'Yes?'

'What are you doing under your desk?'

'Me?'

'You're not hiding, are you?'

'Why would I be hiding?' I say. I wait a moment, hoping that this will satisfy her, but her feet remain where they are. 'I am looking for my stapler,' I add.

'Oh,' Ish says. On one ankle, between her patent-leather pumps and the hem of her skirt, I glimpse a slender chain from which several small animal-charms dangle. Now a pair of brown brogues approaches over the fuzzy blue carpet tiles and come to a halt beside Ish's pumps.

'What's happening?' I hear Jurgen say.

'Claude's looking for his stapler,' Ish says.

'Oh,' says Jurgen, and then, 'But here is his stapler, directly on the desk.'

'So it is,' Ish says. 'Claude, your stapler's right here on your desk!'

I clamber out and to my feet, and look down to where she is pointing. 'Ah!' I say, attempting to appear pleased and surprised.

'Are you coming for lunch?' Jurgen says. 'We are going to the hippie place.'

'I'm a little busy,' I say.

'It's Casual Day!' Ish exhorts me. 'You can't eat at your desk on Casual Day!'

'I've got a meeting with Walter this afternoon.'

'Come on, Claude, you can't live on Carambars.' She grabs my arm and starts tugging me.

Ish studied anthropology back in Australia; Casual Day, as one of the few rituals we have at the Bank of Torabundo, is something she takes very seriously. For most of the staff a pair of well-pressed chinos and perhaps an undone top shirt-button will suffice, but she's wearing a low-cut top fringed with tassels, and a long, multicoloured skirt, also with tassels. She has even topped up her tan for the occasion, a deep greasy brown that makes it look like she has smeared her body with paté. This image, when it occurs to me, immediately makes me nauseous, and as we descend in the elevator my stomach dips and soars like a fairground ride. I dislike Casual Day at the best of times; today it spurs my paranoia to new and queasy heights.

'Is Kevin coming?' I say to distract myself.

'He went on ahead to try and get a table,' Ish says.

'This whole place goes mental on Casual Day,' Jurgen says.

At every floor the elevator stops and we are joined by more people in pressed chinos with their top shirt-button undone, squeezing into the little metal box beside us like clowns into a car in the world's most boring circus. The crush makes my heart race; it's a relief to step through the double-doors of Transaction House and into the

F

fresh air – but only for a moment.

Pastel waves of identically-clad bodies are converging on the plaza from every direction. I scan the approaching faces, the bland gazes that beat against mine. Amid all the smart-casualwear a figure in black should be easy to spot – but that means I too am an obvious target, and in a freezing flash I can picture him, making his way through the sea of bodies, a cancerous cell swimming through the innocent blood.

'Thinking of getting a bidet,' Ish says.

'For the new apartment?' Jurgen says.

'Wasn't something I'd thought of initially, but the bloke from the showroom called up and said because I'm going for the full suite they can throw in a bidet for half-price. The question, do I *want* a bidet? You know, at this stage I've got my toilet routine pretty much worked out.'

'You do not want to feel like an alien in your own bathroom,' Jurgen agrees. 'I suppose Claude would be the expert. Claude, how much of a benefit do you think the addition of a bidet would be?'

'Do you think French people do nothing else but eat baguettes and sit on their bidets?' I snap.

'In Germany, toilets have a special shelf in the bowl,' Jurgen replies equably. 'Meaning that before you flush you have the opportunity to examine...'

I tune him out, return to my search. Above my head, monochrome birds wheel and swoop, like scraps torn from the overcast sky. How long has it been now? A week? Two? That's since I first became conscious of him, though when I think back before that, I seem to find him there too, posed unobtrusively at the back of my memories.

There's no discernable pattern to his appearances; he'll be here one day, somewhere else the next. In the gloom of morning, I might see him by the tram tracks as I make the brief, synaptic journey from my apartment building to the bank; later, bent over a pitchbook with Jurgen, I'll glance out the window and spot him seated on a bench, eating sunflower seeds from a packet. Once I saw him motionless right in the middle of the deserted plaza, counting out the hours like the gnomon of a sundial. In the deli, in the bar – even at night, when I stand on my balcony and look out over the depopulated concourse, I will seem to glimpse him for an instant in a darkened window, his blank gaze trained on me like a gunsight.

The Ark is in sight now; I can see the waitresses gliding back and forth inside, the customers eating, talking, toying with their phones. Of my pursuer there is no sign, yet with every step I am overcome with the dreadful certainty *that he is in there*. I stall, with a clammy mouth begin to mumble excuses, but too late! The door is opening and a figure coming towards us—

'Full,' Kevin says.

'Balls,' Ish says.

F

'They're saying fifteen minutes,' Kevin says.

Jurgen looks at his watch. 'That would give us only twelve and a half minutes to eat.'

'Oh well,' I say, with a false sigh. 'I suppose we must go back to—'

'What about that new place?' Ish says, snapping her fingers. 'Over on the other side of the square? You'll like it, Claude, it's French.'

The 'new place' is called Chomps Elysées. An image of the Eiffel Tower adorns the laminated sign, and on the walls inside are photographs of Sacré-Cœur and the Moulin Rouge. Beyond that, nothing about it seems especially French. I don't mind; I'm just happy to be clear of the Ark. I order a mochaccino and something called a 'Panini Fromage', and while Kevin offers his opinions on Ish's lavatorial dilemma, I sit back in my seat and tell myself to relax. Who would be interested in following me? Nobody, is the answer. Nobody outside my department even knows I exist.

This thought doesn't cheer me quite as I intended it to; and the Panini Fromage, when it comes, only makes matters worse. It is not that the cheese tastes bad, exactly; rather, that it tastes of *nothing*. I have never tasted *nothing* quite so strongly before. It's like eating a tiny black hole wrapped in an Italian sandwich. There is no way food this bad would ever be served in Paris, I think to myself, and experience a sudden stab of homesickness at the thought of how far behind I have left my native city and everyone I loved. Now with every chew I feel the emptiness rising inside, as if, like a kind of anti-madeleine, the panini were cancelling my past, leaving me with nothing but my life as it is here, today, in all its grey anaesthesia...

I approach the counter. The waitress's scowl appears authentically Parisian, but her accent, when she speaks, denotes the more energetic hostility of the Slav.

'Yes?' she says, not pretending that my appearance has made her any less bored.

'I think there has been a mistake,' I say.

'Panini Fromage,' she says. 'Is French cheese.'

'But it is not cheese,' I say. 'It's artificial.'

'Artificial?'

'Not real.'

Prising apart the bread for her inspection, I point at the off-white slab sitting atop the melancholy lettuce. It resembles nothing so much as a blank piece of matter, featureless and opaque, before God's brush has painted it with the colour and shape of specificity. 'I am from France,' I tell her, as if this might clarify things. 'And this is not French cheese.'

The girl looks at me with unconcealed contempt. You are not supposed to complain in restaurants like this one; you are not supposed to notice the food in restaurants like this one, any more than you are supposed to notice the streets you hurry through, latte in hand, back to your computer. The computer screen, the telephone, that disembodied world is the one we truly inhabit; the Financial Services Centre is merely a frame for it, a sketched outline, the equivalent of the chalk marks of a child's game on the pavement.

'You vant chench?' the waitress taunts: I raise my hands in surrender, and, cheeks burning, turn away.

Only then do I realise the man in black is standing right behind me.

Around us, the café has returned to normal life; the sullen girl rings up another panini, the office workers drink their uniquely-tailored coffees. I goggle at Ish at the nearby table, but she doesn't seem to notice – nor does anyone else, as if he had cast some cloak of invisibility over us. Blinding white light pours through the open door; he gazes at me, his eyes a terrifying ice-blue.

'Claude,' he says. He knows my name, of course he does.

'What do you want from me?' I try to sound defiant, but my voice will not come in more than a whisper.

'Just to talk,' he says.

'You have the wrong man,' I say. 'I have not done anything.'

'That makes you the right man,' he says with a smile. 'That makes you exactly the right man.'

❡ His name is Paul; he is a writer. 'I've been shadowing you for a project I'm working on. I had no idea you'd spotted me. I hope I didn't alarm you.'

'I was not alarmed,' I lie. 'Although these days, as a banker, you have to be very careful.'

'Well, I can only apologise again. And lunch is definitely on me – ah, here we go.' The waitress appears, dark and genial as her counterpart in the fake French café was blonde and cold, and sets down two bowls of freshly-made sorrel soup. We are back in the Ark, this time having secured a table.

'I can see why you like this place,' he says, dipping a hunk of bread into his soup. 'The food's fantastic. And I love all this nautical stuff,' nodding at the portholes, the great anchor by the door. 'It's like going on a boat ride.' He purses his lips and blows on the bread; he doesn't appear to be in any great hurry to tell me why we are here.

'So you're a writer,' I say. 'What kind of things do you write?'

'A few years back I wrote a novel,' he says, 'called FOR LOVE OF A CLOWN.'

This prompts a faint ringing at the back of my mind – some kind of prize...?

'You're thinking of THE CLOWNS OF SORROW by Bimal Banerjee, that won the Raytheon. My novel came out around the same time, similar enough subject matter. It did okay, but when the time came to begin the next one, I found I'd hit a kind of wall. Started asking myself some tough questions – what's a novel for, what place does it have in the modern world, all that. For a long time I was stuck, well and truly stuck.

Then out of nowhere it came to me. Idea for a new book, the whole thing right there, like a baby left on the doorstep.'

'And what's it about?' I ask politely.

'What's it about.' Paul smiles. 'Well, it's about you, Claude. It's about you.'

I am too surprised to conceal it. 'Me?'

'I've been studying you and your daily routine for a number of weeks now. It seems to me that your life embodies certain values, certain fundamental features of our modern world. We're living in a time of great change, and a man like you is right at the coalface of that change.'

'I do not think my life would make a very interesting book,' I say. 'I feel I can speak with a certain amount of authority here.'

He laughs. 'Well, in a way, that's the point. That's what my crisis of faith was about. The stories we read in books, what's presented to us as being interesting – they have very little to do with real life as it's lived today. I'm not just talking about straight–up escapism either, your vampires, serial killers, codes hidden in paintings and so on. I mean so–called serious literature. A boy goes hunting with his emotion-ally volatile father, a bereaved woman befriends an asylum–seeker, a composer with a rare neurological disorder walks around New York, thinking about the nature of art. People looking back over their lives, people having revelations, people discover-ing meaning. *Meaning*, that's the big thing. The way these books have it, you trip over a rock you'll find some hidden meaning waiting there. Everyone's constantly on the verge of some soul–shaking transformation. And it's – if you'll forgive my language – it's bullshit. In real life, people go to work and they come home and they watch TV and they go to bed and that's it. If they think at all it's, do I want steak or pie? Has the waitress forgotten my order? Where's a good place for a holiday? Did the boss not like that joke? They don't transform, they don't stop to smell the roses, they don't sit around recollecting long passages of their childhood – Jesus, I don't know about you, but I can hardly remember what I was doing two hours ago.'

'So you want to write a book that... has no meaning?'

'I want to write a book that isn't full of things that only ever happen in books,' he says. 'I want to write something that genuinely reflects how people live today. Real, actual life, not some ivory–tower palaver, not a whole load of *literature*. What's it like to be alive in the twenty–first century? Look at this place, for example.' He sweeps an arm at the window, filled with the glass anonymity of the International Financial Services Centre. 'We're in the middle of Dublin, two minutes' walk from where Joyce set *ULYSSES*. But it doesn't look like Dublin. It doesn't look like *anywhere*. We could be in London, or Frankfurt, or Kuala Lumpur. There are all these people, but nobody's speaking to each other, everyone's just looking at their phones. This whole place is about being somewhere else. And *that's* modern life.'

F

'I see,' I say, although I don't, quite.

'So the question is, how do you describe it? If James Joyce was writing about Dublin today, if he was writing not about some nineteenth-century backwater but about the capital of the most globalised country in the world – where would he begin? Who would his Bloom be? His Everyman?'

He looks at me pointedly, but it takes me a moment to realise his import.

'You think I am an Everyman?'

He makes a *hey presto* gesture with his hands.

'But I'm not even Irish,' I protest. 'How can I be your typical Dubliner?'

He shakes his head vigorously. 'That's key. Like I said, *somewhere else* is what this place is all about. Think about it, in your work, you have colleagues from all over the place, right?'

'That's true.'

'And the cleaning staff are from all over the place, and the waitresses in this restaurant are from all over the place. Modern life is a centrifuge, it throws people in every direction. That's why you're so perfect for this book. The Everyman's uprooted, he's alone, he's separated from his friends and family. And the work that you do – you're a banker, isn't that so?'

'Yes, an analyst at the Bank of Torabundo,' I say, before it occurs to me how strange it is that he knows this.

'Well, I hardly need to say how representative that is. The story of the twenty-first century so far is the story of the banks. Look at the mess this country's in because of them, for a start.'

'So your book will be a kind of exposé,' I say neutrally.

'No, no, no,' he waves his hands as if to dispel some evil-smelling smoke. 'I don't want to write a takedown. I'm not interested in demonising the whole industry because of the actions of a minority. I want to get past the stereotypes. I want to discover the humanity inside the corporate machine. I want to show what it's like to be a modern man, and this is where modern man lives, not on a fishing trawler, not in a coal mine, not on a ranch in Wyoming. This,' he gestures once again at the window, and we both turn in our seats to contemplate the reticular expanse of the Centre, the blank façades of the multinationals – 'is where modern life *comes from*. The feel of it, the look of it. Everything. What happens inside those buildings defines how we live our lives. Even if people only notice when it goes wrong. The banks are like the heart, the engine room, the world-within-the-world. The stuff that comes out of these places,' whirling a finger again at the Centre, 'the credit, the loans, that's what our reality is *made of*. They're the pages we write our lives on. So, with that in mind, can you think of a *better* subject for a book – than you?'

❡ Essentially, he tells me, the process would be a more intensive version of what he's doing already: following me around, observing at close quarters, focussing, as much as is possible, on my work for the bank.

'What would I have to do?'

'You wouldn't have to do anything,' Paul says. 'Just be yourself. Just be.' He glances at the bill, takes a note from his wallet and lays it on the table. 'I don't expect you to make a decision like this on the spot. To lay yourself out for a perfect stranger – that's a big thing to ask. I wish I could say you'd be handsomely rewarded, but right now all I can offer is the dubious honour of providing material for a book that might never get published.' He cracks a grin. 'Still, I bet the girls in the office'll be interested to find out you're a character in a work of fiction!'

'How do you mean?'

'Well, think about Heathcliff, Mr Darcy. Captain Ahab, even. Women go nuts for them.'

'All those characters are imaginary,' I say slowly.

'Exactly. But *you'll* be real. Do you see? It's like you'll be getting the best of both worlds.'

As if to bear out his words, the beautiful dark-haired waitress flashes me a smile as she glides past. My head is spinning, and it really is time for me to get back to the office. But there is still one question he has not answered. 'Why me? There are thirty thousand people working in the Financial Services Centre. Why did you choose me?'

'To be honest, that's what's caught my eye initially,' he says.

'That. Oh,' I realise, he's pointing at my jacket, which I am in the course of slipping back on.

'The black really stands out, especially with the tie. Most people here go for grey. Must be a French thing, is it?'

'Yes,' I say, 'it's a French thing.'

'Makes you look very literary,' he says. 'And when I got closer I could see you had a certain... I don't know, a sensibility. I got the impression that you were different from the others. That you weren't just going through the motions. That you were searching for something, maybe. It's hard to explain.' He rips a scrap of paper from a little red notebook and scribbles down his number. 'Look,' he says. 'I could be completely wrong, but I think there's a really important book to be written about this place. And I think you'd be perfect for it. If it doesn't feel right to you for whatever reason, I promise, I'll disappear from your life. But can I ask you at least to think about it?'

¶ 'Here he is!' Jurgen says as I enter the research department. 'We were beginning to think we must send out the search party!'

'Where'd you disappear to?' Ish inquires, through a mouthful of paperclips.

'Nowhere,' I shrug. 'I ran into someone and went for a coffee.'

F

'Casual Day,' Jurgen shakes his head. 'Anything can happen.'

Kimberlee comes in from reception. 'Claude, Ryan Colchis called about some numbers on a Ukrainian outfit you were digging up for him?'

'Okay,' I say.

'And Walter's PA called to say he's coming in.'

'There goes your weekend,' Ish says.

I go to my terminal, confront the wall of fresh emails. Already the writer and his strange proposal are beginning to seem unreal, one of those hazy episodes you can't be sure you didn't dream. And yet the familiar objects of the office have acquired a curious sheen – appear to *resonate* somehow, like enchanted furniture in a fairytale that will dance around the room as soon as you turn your back...

'Hey, has Claude heard the news?' Kevin calls from his desk.

'What news?' I say, with a curious feeling of – what, synchronicity? As though someone is looking over my shoulder?

'Blankly's the new CEO,' Ish says. 'Rachael's office just sent down word.'

'Blankly got it,' I say. 'Well, well.'

'Things will be changing, Claude,' Jurgen says. 'This is the whole new beginning of the Bank of Torabundo story.'

'Yes,' I say, and then, 'I should call Colchis.'

'Are you feeling better?' Ish catches my arm. 'You looked a bit off earlier?'

'Yes, yes, I just needed some air,' I tell her, but she is not deterred: she continues to scrutinise me. 'Are you sure?' she says. 'You seem, I dunno, different somehow?'

'Claude is never different,' Jurgen says, clapping me on the shoulder. 'Claude is always the same.'

'Yeah...' Ish wrinkles her nose thoughtfully; and I hurry away to my desk, as if I have a secret to keep.

❡ The Pareto principle, also known as the 80–20 rule, is one of the first things you learn in banking. For any given area of life, 80 per cent of the effects come from 20 per cent of the causes: thus 80 per cent of your profits come from 20 per cent of your clients, 80 per cent of your time is spent with 20 per cent of your friends, 80 per cent of your music listening is from 20 per cent of your library, etc. The idea is to minimise the 'grey zone' that devours your day, the 80 per cent of your reading, for instance, that yields only 20 per cent of your information.

Walter Corless is very much aware what side of the rule he's on. He knows he is the wealthiest and most powerful man you have ever met, and as such he demands 100 per cent of your time and attention. A meeting with or even a call from Walter is like having some supermassive planet materialise in your little patch of space – blocking the sun, overwhelming your own gravitational field so that you can only watch as the entire structure of your world goes hurtling off to rearrange itself on his. He started off selling turf from the back of a flatbed truck; thirty years later, he is CEO of one of the biggest construction companies in the British Isles. Even the worldwide slump hasn't hurt him: while his peers put all their chips into housing, Dublex diversified into transport, logistics, and, most profitably, high-security developments – military compounds, fortifications, prisons – which, as crisis sweeps across Europe and Asia, constitute a rare growth area. That a company he named after his daughter now builds enhanced interrogation facilities in Belarus gives a good indication of the man's attitudes to business and life in general. (That daughter), Lexi, now runs a string of nursing homes known informally as the Glue Factory.

His driver calls me shortly after six; I go outside to find Walter's limo parked – in contravention of all of the Centre's rules – on the plaza in front of Transaction House. Walter is sprawled across the back seat. He stares at me as I squeeze into the fold-down seat opposite him, breathing heavily through his nose. He is a dour, grey-faced man, who looks rather like he was dug up from the same bog he got his first bags of turf. Newspaper profiles will refer to his 'drive' and his 'focus', but these are euphemisms. What Walter has is the dead-eyed relentlessness of the killer in a horror movie, the kind that lumbers after you inexorably, heedless of knives or bullets. His fortune runs into the billions, and he employs a team of accountants in tax havens around the world, but he still enjoys calling to his debtors personally, and the pockets of his coat are always full of cheques and bank drafts. Sometimes he'll present me with a fistful, with instructions to invest them in this or that. This is not strictly my job, but then Walter doesn't care what my job is; or rather, as our biggest client, he knows that my job is whatever he says it is.

Tonight he wants to ask my thoughts on a tender. Dublex has been approached by the interior ministry of the Middle Eastern autocracy of Oran to fortify the private compound of the Caliph. 'They are expecting trouble?'

Walter just grunts. He knows, of course; he has specialists in every conceivable field, but he still likes to canvas opinions from as wide a spectrum as possible before making a decision, in order, Ish says, to maximise the number of people he can yell at afterwards. 'Is there money in this fucker's pocket, is what I'm asking you,' he says.

'It's one of the biggest oil producers in the region, I imagine his credit is good,' I say. Walter scowls. I tell him I'll look into it, and he signals his approval by changing the subject, launching into a familiar tirade about 'regulations', although as Ish likes to point out, though not to his face, the only way Ireland could have a less regulated environment would be if they switched off the gravity.

It's after nine when I get back to the apartment and can finally revisit my lunch-time encounter. Searching online, I discover that the novel he mentioned, *FOR LOVE OF A CLOWN*, is real; an image search confirms, in a picture that shows him shaking hands with a man dressed as a papaya at something called the Donard Exotic Fruits and Book Festival, that its author and the man who approached me are one and the same. His Apeiron page has a handful of customer write-ups, both negative: the first compares his clown-themed novel to Bimal Banerjee's, and awards it a rating of two snakes and a cactus; the second gives no rating at all, and consists solely of the line, 'On no account should you lend money to this man'.

Beyond that, there is nothing; as far as the wider world is concerned, for the last seven years Paul might as well not have existed. This is consistent with what he said about hitting a wall. Still I can't help wondering if I imagined the whole thing. Life in the Financial Services Centre often leaves that impression.

I go onto my balcony, try to look out with the eyes of a novelist. Over the rooftops, I can see the cold point of the Spire jut up into the darkness, like a radio transmitter from the heart of things: but it is only on rare evenings, when the wind is blowing in a particular direction, that I hear its broadcasts – the whoops, the screams, the laughter and fights, and even then only faintly, like the revelry of ghosts. Usually, when night has fallen and only a few lights remain chequering the dark slabs of the buildings, it is easy, looking out over the pristine, deserted concourses, to believe the world has upped stakes and gone, followed the baton of trade west, leaving me here alone.

F

SPONSORS

LES BIJOUX

COQUEƎE

bijouxcoquette.com

(your words here)

There's a long history of writing women *(writers)* off. It's time to right that wrong, to get relevant not relegated.

Visualizing is for the work. **Galvanizing** is for getting the work out there. We can see your words here. So can publishers, agents + scholars. **Can you?**

Until it's just about the art.
Submit your literary work now.

PEN + BRUSH
www.penandbrush.org

PIÑA — PINEAPPLE
COCO — COCONUT
MELON — CANTALOUPE
FRESA — STRAWBERRY
LIMON — LEMON
CIRUELA — PLUM
PLATANO — BANANA
SANDIA — WATERMELON
MANGO — MANGO
TAMARINDO — TAMARIN
DURAZNO — PEACH
CHOCOLATE — CHOCOLATE
CHAMOY — CHAMOY
MANGOYADAS — MANGOYADAS
GUAYAVA — GUAVA
UVA — GRAPE
ROMPOPE — EGGNOG
VAINILLA — VANILLA
NUEZ — PECAN

Lynette Yiadom-Boakye
A Radical Under Beechwood, 2015
Oil on canvas, 80 x 70 cm

Corvi-Mora
1a Kempsford Road, London, SE11 4NU
 +44 (0)20 7840 9111
www.corvi-mora.com

OHWOW

Torey Thornton
Be Right Back, and Left, 2015
Metallic paint, acrylic and foam core on wood panel
96 x 82 inches / 243.8 x 208.3 cm

www.oh-wow.com

NOON

A LITERARY ANNUAL

1324 LEXINGTON AVENUE   PMB 298   NEW YORK NY 10128

EDITION PRICE $12 DOMESTIC $17 FOREIGN

APPENDIX

ANNA ASLANYAN is is a journalist and translator. She writes for a number of publications – including *3:AM MAGAZINE*, the *TLS*, the *INDEPENDENT* and the *LRB* blog – mainly about literature and arts. Her translations from Russian include *POST-POST SOVIET? ART, POLITICS AND SOCIETY IN RUSSIA AT THE TURN OF THE DECADE*, a collection of essays focused on Russia's contemporary art scene.

FEDERICO CAMPAGNA is a co-founder of the Milanese street-poetry collective Eveline. Since moving to London he has worked at the Max Wigram contemporary art gallery, at the publishing workers' cooperative Zed Books, and at Verso Books, where he currently holds the position of rights manager. In 2009 he started a long-term collaboration with Franco 'Bifo' Berardi, whose reader he is currently editing for the Italian publisher Il Saggiatore. In 2012 he co-edited *WHAT WE ARE FIGHTING FOR* (Pluto Press) and in 2013 published *THE LAST NIGHT - ANTI-WORK, ATHEISM, ADVENTURE* (Zero Books).

JON DAY is a writer, academic and cyclist. He worked as a bicycle courier in London for several years, and now teaches English Literature at King's College London. He writes for the *LONDON REVIEW OF BOOKS*, *n+1* and *APOLLO*, and is a regular book critic for the *FINANCIAL TIMES* and the *TELEGRAPH*. He is a contributing editor of *THE JUNKET*. His book *CYCLOGEOGRAPHY* is forthcoming from Notting Hill Editions.

CAITE DOLIN-LEACH is a writer and translator. She lives in Cape Town, South Africa.

JORIE GRAHAM is the author of numerous collections of poetry, most recently *PLACE* (2012), *SEA CHANGE* (Ecco, 2008), *NEVER* (2002), *SWARM* (2000), and *THE DREAM OF THE UNIFIED FIELD*: *SELECTED POEMS 1974-1994*, which won the 1996 Pulitzer prize for poetry. Her newest collection is *FROM THE NEW WORLD* (*POEMS 1976-2014*). She teaches at Harvard University.

PATRICK LANGLEY is a contributing editor at *THE WHITE REVIEW*.

EDOUARD LEVÉ, a writer, photographer and visual artist, was the author of four books – *ŒUVRES*, *NEWSPAPER*, *AUTOPORTRAIT* and *SUICIDE* – and three books of photographs. *SUICIDE*, published in 2008, was his last book.

PAUL MURRAY studied English and Philosophy at Trinity College, Dublin, and creative writing at the University of East Anglia. His first novel, *AN EVENING OF LONG GOODBYES*, was shortlisted for the Whitbread Prize in 2003 and was nominated for the Kerry Group Irish Fiction Award. *SKIPPY DIES*, his second novel, was shortlisted for the Costa prize and was a finalist for the National Book Critics Circle Award. *THE MARK AND THE VOID*, excerpted in this issue, will be published by Hamish Hamilton in July 2015.

HELEN OYEYEMI is the author of five novels, including *WHITE IS FOR WITCHING*, which won a 2010 Somerset Maugham Award, *MR FOX*, and *BOY, SNOW, BIRD*. She was named on the *GRANTA* 2013 Best of Young British Novelists' list.

HOLLY PESTER is a poet and multidisciplinary writer. She has worked as an archivist, lecturer and practice–based researcher with readings, performances and sound installations featuring at Segue, New York, dOCUMENTA 13, Whitechapel Gallery, and the Serpentine Galleries. She teaches courses on Oulipo and Poetic Practice at the University of Essex. Her collection *GO TO RECEPTION AND ASK FOR SARA IN RED FELT TIP* is coming out with Book Works in April 2015.

ORLANDO READE is writing a Ph.D. on English poetry and theories of matter in the seventeenth century. His 'Notes on an Unfamiliar Poetry' was published in *THE WHITE REVIEW NO.5*.

LUKE RUDOLF is an artist based in London, represented by Kate MacGarry Gallery. His work is exhibited in The National Gallery of Victoria, Melbourne, at the Saatchi Collection, and the Zabludowicz Collection, both in London.

JAN STEYN is a translator and critic. He lives in Cape Town, South Africa.

J. S. TENNANT works for PEN International, *THE WHITE REVIEW* and *ASYMPTOTE*.

PATRICIA TREIB born in 1979, lives and works in Brooklyn. Selected group exhibitions include *MODERN TALKING* at the Cluj Museum, Cluj, Romania (2012); *EXPANDED PAINTING*, Prague Biennale 5, Prague, Czech Republic (2011); *BESIDES, WITH, AGAINST, AND YET: ABSTRACTION AND THE READY-MADE GESTURE* – curated by Debra Singer, The Kitchen (2009). Solo exhibitions have been held at Tibor de Nagy Gallery (2012) and John Connelly Presents (2008). Treib was a 2013 MacDowell Colony Fellow and a Marie Walsh Sharpe Foundation grantee in 2007.

ENRIQUE VILA-MATAS was born in Barcelona in 1948. His works include *BARTLEBY & CO*, *MONTANO*, *NEVER ANY END TO PARIS*, *THE VERTICAL JOURNEY*, winner of the Premio Romulo Gallegos, and *DUBLINESQUE*, which was shortlisted for the 2013 Independent Foreign Fiction Prize.

DAISUKE YOKOTA is a Japanese artist. He is the recipient of the first award from the Foam Outset Exhibition Fund. He lives and works in Tokyo, Japan.

FRIENDS OF THE WHITE REVIEW